Alexandre Dumas (24 July 1802 – 5 December 1870), also known as Alexandre Dumas père (French for 'father'), was a French writer. His works have been translated into many languages, and he is one of the most widely read French authors. Many of his historical novels of high adventure were originally published as serials, including The Count of Monte Cristo, The Three Musketeers, Twenty Years After, and The Vicomte of Bragelonne: Ten Years Later. His novels have been adapted since the early twentieth century for nearly 200 films. Dumas' last novel, The Knight of Sainte-Hermine, unfinished at his death, was completed by scholar Claude Schopp and published in 2005. It was published in English in 2008 as The Last Cavalier. Prolific in several genres, Dumas began his career by writing plays, which were successfully produced from the first. He also wrote numerous magazine articles and travel books; his published works totalled 100,000 pages. In the 1840s, Dumas founded the Théâtre Historique in Paris. (Source: Wikipedia)

Literary works:
The Three Musketeers
Twenty Years After
The Vicomte of Bragelonne
Ten Years Later
Louise de la Valliere
The Man in the Iron Mask
The Count of Monte Cristo
The Women's War
The Pale Lady
The Black Tulip
Olympe de Cleves
Isaac Laquedem
Catherine Blum
Georges
Amaury

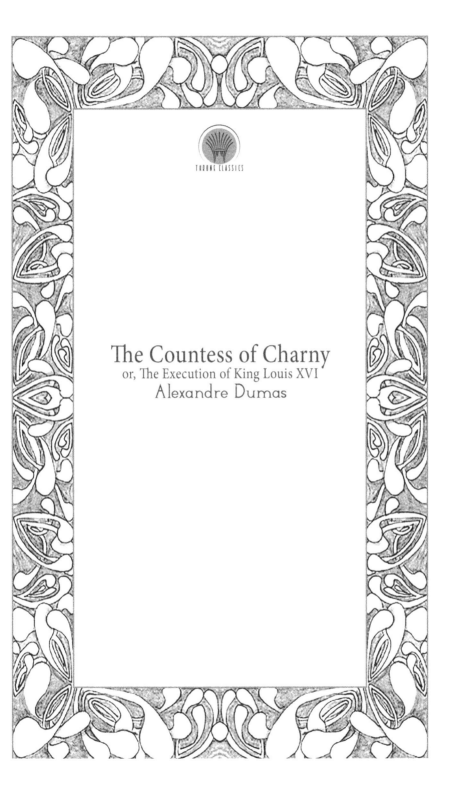

THRONE CLASSICS

The Countess of Charny
or, The Execution of King Louis XVI
Alexandre Dumas

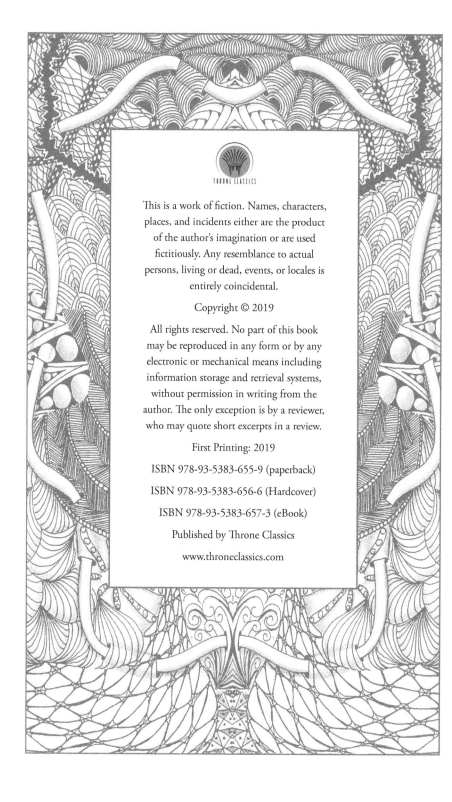

First Printing: 2019

ISBN 978-93-5383-655-9 (paperback)

ISBN 978-93-5383-656-6 (Hardcover)

ISBN 978-93-5383-657-3 (eBook)

Published by Throne Classics

www.throneclassics.com

Contents

The Countess of Charny
or, The Execution of King Louis XVI

CHAPTER I. THE NEW MEN AT THE WHEEL.

It was on the first of October, 1791, that the new Legislative Assembly was to be inaugurated over France.

King Louis XVI., captured with Queen Marie Antoinette and the royal family, while attempting to escape from the kingdom and join his brothers and the other princes abroad, was held in a kind of detention, like imprisonment without hard labor, in the Tuileries Palace in Paris.

His fate hung on the members of the new House of Representatives. Let us hasten to see what they were.

The Congress was composed of seven hundred and forty-five members: four hundred lawyers of one kind or another; some seventy literary men; seventy priests who had taken the oath to abide by the Constitution, not yet framed, but to which the king had subscribed on the sketch. The remaining two hundred odd were landholders, farming their own estates or hiring them out to others.

Among these was François Billet, a robust peasant of forty-five, distinguished by the people of Paris and France as a hero, from having been mainly instrumental in the taking of the Bastile, regarded as the embodiment of the ancient tyranny, now almost leveled with the dust.

Billet had suffered two wrongs at the hands of the king's men and the nobles, which he had sworn to avenge as well on the classes as on the individuals.

His farm-house had been pillaged by Paris policemen acting under a blank warrant signed by the king and issued at the request of Andrea de Taverney, Countess of Charny, the queen's favorite, as her husband the count was reckoned, too. She had a spite against Billet's friend, Dr. Honore Gilbert, a noted patriot and politician. In his youth, this afterward distinguished physician had taken advantage of her senses being steeped in a mesmeric swoon, to lower her pride. Thanks to this trance and from his overruling love, he was the progenitor of her son, Sebastian Emile Gilbert; but with all the pride of this paternity, he was haunted by unceasing remorse. Andrea could not forgive this crime, all the more as it was a thorn in her side since her marriage.

It was a marriage enforced on her, as the Count of Charny had been caught by the king on his knees to the queen; and to prevent the stupid monarch being convinced by this scene that there was truth in the tattle at court that Count Charny was Marie Antoinette's paramour, she had explained that he merely was suing for the hand of her friend Andrea. The king's consent given, this marriage took place, but for six years the couple dwelt apart; not that mutual love did not prevail between them, but neither was aware of the affection each had inspired in the other at first sight.

The new countess thought that Charny's affection for the queen was a guilty and durable one; while he, believing his wife, by compulsion, a saint on earth, dared not presume on the position which fate and devotion to their sovereign had imposed on them both.

This devotion was confirmed on the count's part, cemented by blood; for his two brothers, Valence and Isidore, had lost their lives in defending the king and queen from the revolutionists.

Andrea had a brother, Philip, who also loved the queen, but he had been offended by her amour with Charny; and, being touched by an American republican fever while fighting with Lafayette for the liberation of the thirteen colonies, he had quitted the court of France.

On his way he had wounded Gilbert, whom he learned to be his sister's wronger, as well as having stolen away her infant son; but although the wound would have been mortal under other treatment, it had been healed by the wondrous medicaments of Joseph Balsamo, alias Count Cagliostro, the celebrated head of the Invisibles, a branch of the Orient Freemasons, dedicated to overthrow the monarchy and set up a republic, after the United States model, in France, if not in Europe.

Gilbert and Cagliostro were therefore fast friends, to say nothing of the latter's regret that he should have set temptation in the young man's way; it was he who had plunged Andrea into the magnetic slumber from which she had awakened a maid no longer.

But some recompense had come to the proud lady, after the six years' wedded life to the very man she adored, though fate and misunderstanding had estranged them. On learning what a martyr she had been through the unconscious motherhood, Count George had more than forgiven her—he worshiped her; and in their country seat at Boursonnes, eighteen miles from Paris, he was forgetting, in her lovely arms the demands of his queen, his king, and his caste, to use his influence in the political arena.

This silence on his part led to the candidature of Farmer Billet being unimpeded.

Besides, Charny would hardly have moved in opposition to the latter, as one cause of the enmity of the peasant was his daughter's ruin by Viscount Isidore Charny. The death of the latter, not being by Billet's hand, had not appeased the grudge. He was a stern, unrelenting man; and just as he would not forgive his daughter Catherine for her dishonor, or even look upon her son, he stood out uncompromisingly against the nobles and the priests.

Charny had stolen his daughter; the clergy, in the person of his parish priest, Father Fortier, had refused burial to his wife.

On her grave he had vowed eternal hostility to the nobles and the clericals.

The farmers had great power at election time, as they employed ten, twenty, or thirty hands; and though the suffrage was divided into two classes at the period, the result depended on the rural vote.

As each man quitted Billet at the grave, he shook him by the hand, saying:

"It is a sure thing, brother."

Billet had gone home to his lonely farm, easy on this score; for the first time he saw a plain way of returning the noble class and royalty all the harm they had done him. He felt, but did not reason, and his thirst for vengeance was as blind as the blows he had received.

His daughter had come home to nurse her mother, and receive at the last gasp her blessing and for her son, born in shame; but Billet had said never a word to her; none could tell if he were aware of her flitting through the farm. Since a year he had not uttered her name, and it was the same as if she had never existed.

Her only friend was Ange Pitou, a poor peasant lad whom Billet had harbored when he was driven from home by his Aunt Angelique.

As Catherine was really the ruler of the roast on the farm, it was but natural that Pitou should offer her some part of the gratitude Billet had earned. This excellent feeling expanded into love; but there was little chance for the peasant when the girl had been captivated by the elegant young lord, although the elevation common during revolution had exalted Ange into a captaincy of the National Guards.

But Pitou had never swerved in his love for the deluded girl. He had a heart of gold; he was deeply sorry that Catherine had not loved him, but on comparing himself with young Charny, he acknowledged that she must prefer him. He envied Isidore, but he bore Catherine no ill-will; quite otherwise, he still loved her with profound and entire devotion.

To say this dedication was completely exempt from anguish, is going too far; but the pangs which made Pitou's heart ache at each new token of Catherine's love for her dead lover, showed his ineffable goodness.

All his feeling for Catherine when Isidore was slain at Varennes, where Billet arrested the king in his flight, was of utter pity. Quite contrary to Billet, he did justice to the young noble in the way of grace, generosity, and kindness, though he was his rival without knowing it. Like Catherine, he knew that the barriers of caste were insurmountable, and that the viscount could not have made his sweetheart his wife.

The consequence was that Pitou perhaps more loved the widow in her sorrow than when she was the coquettish girl, but it came to pass that he almost loved the little orphan boy like his own.

Let none be astonished, therefore, that after taking leave of Billet like the others, Ange went toward Haramont instead of Billet's farm, which might also be his home.

But he had lodgings at Haramont village, where he was born, and he was chief of the National Guards there.

They were so accustomed to his sudden departures and unexpected returns, that nobody was worried at them. When he went away, they said to one another: "He has gone to town to confer with General Lafayette," for the French lieutenant of General Washington was the friend, here as there, of Dr. Gilbert, who was their fellow-peasants' patron, and had furnished the funds to equip the Haramont company of volunteers.

On their commander's return they asked news of the capital; and as he could give the freshest and truest, thanks to Dr. Gilbert, who was an honorary physician to the king as well as friend of Cagliostro—in other words, the communicator between the two Leyden jars of the revolution—Pitou's predictions were sure to be realized in a few days, so that all continued to show him blind trust, as well as military captain as political prophet.

On his part, Gilbert knew all that was good and self-sacrificing in the peasant; he felt that he was a man to whom he might at the scratch intrust his life or Sebastian's—a treasure or a commission, anything confided to strength and loyalty. Every time Pitou came to Paris, the doctor would ask him if he stood in need of anything, without the young man coloring up; and while he would always say, "Nothing, thank you, Doctor Gilbert," this did not prevent the physician giving him some money, which Pitou ingulfed in his pocket.

A few gold pieces, with what he picked up in the game shot or trapped in the Duke of Orleans' woods, were a fortune; so, rarely did he find himself at the end of his resources when he met the doctor and had his supply renewed.

Knowing, then, how friendly Pitou was with Catherine and her baby, it will be understood that he hastily separated from Billet, to know how his cast-off daughter was getting on.

His road to Haramont took him past a hut in the woods where lived a veteran of the wars, who, on a pension and the privilege of killing a hare or a rabbit each day, lived a happy hermit's life, remote from man. Father Clovis, as this old soldier was called, was a great friend of Pitou. He had taught the boy to go gunning, and also the military drill by which he had trained the Haramont Guards to be the envy of the county. When Catherine was banished from her father's, after Billet had tried to shoot Isidore, his hut sheltered her till after the birth of her son. On her applying once more for the like hospitality, he had not hesitated; and when Pitou came along, she was sitting on the bed, with tears on her cheek at the revival of sad memories, and her boy in her arms.

On seeing the new-comer, Catherine set down the child and offered her forehead for Pitou's kiss; he gladly took her two hands, kissed her, and the child was sheltered by the arch formed with his stooping figure. Dropping on his knees to her and kissing the baby's little hands, he exclaimed:

"Never mind, I am rich; Master Isidore shall never come to want."

Pitou had twenty-five gold louis, which he reckoned to make him rich. Keen of wit and kind of heart, Catherine appreciated all that is good.

"Thank you, Captain Pitou," she said; "I believe you, and I am happy in so believing, for you are my only friend, and if you were to cast me off, we should stand alone in the world; but you never will, will you?"

"Oh, don't talk like that," cried Pitou, sobbing; "you will make me pour out all the tears in my body."

"I was wrong; excuse me," she said.

"No, no, you are right; I am a fool to blubber."

"Captain Pitou," said Catherine, "I should like an airing. Give me your arm for a stroll under the trees. I fancy it will do me good."

"I feel as if I were smothering myself," added Pitou.

The child had no need of air, nothing but sleep; so he was laid abed, and

Catherine walked out with Pitou.

Five minutes after they were in the natural temple, under the huge trees.

Without being a philosopher on a level with Voltaire or Rousseau, Pitou understood that he and Catherine were atoms carried on by the whirlwind. But these atoms had their joy and grief just like the other atoms called king, queen, nobles; the mill of God, held by fatality, ground crowns and thrones to dust at the same time, and crushed Catherine's happiness no less harshly than if she wore a diadem.

Two years and a half before, Pitou was a poor peasant lad, hunted from home by his Aunt Angelique, received by Billet, feasted by Catherine, and "cut out" by Isidore.

At present, Ange Pitou was a power; he wore a sword by his side and epaulets on his shoulders; he was called a captain, and he was protecting the widow and son of the slain Viscount Isidore.

Relatively to Pitou the expression was exact of Danton, who, when asked why he was making the revolution, replied: "To put on high what was undermost, and send the highest below all."

But though these ideas danced in his head, he was not the one to profit by them, and the good and modest fellow went on his knees to beg Catherine to let him shield her and the boy.

Like all suffering hearts, Catherine had a finer appreciation in grief than in joy. Pitou, who was in her happy days a lad of no consequence, became the holy creature he really was; in other words, a man of goodness, candor, and devotion. The result was that, unfortunate and in want of a friend, she understood that Pitou was just the friend she wished; and so, always received by Catherine with one hand held out to him, and a witching smile, Pitou began to lead a life of bliss of which he never had had the idea even in dreams of paradise.

During this time, Billet, still mute as regarded his daughter, pursued his idea of being nominated for the House while getting in his harvest.

Only one man could have beaten him, if he had the same ambition; but, entirely absorbed in his love and happiness, the Count of Charny, the world forgetting, believed himself forgotten by the world. He did not think of the matter, enjoying his unexpected felicity.

Hence, nothing opposed Billet's election in Villers Cotterets district, and he was elected by an immense majority.

As soon as chosen, he began to turn everything into money; it had been a good year. He set aside his landlord's share, reserved his own, put aside the grain for sowing, and the fodder for his live stock, and the cash to keep the work-folks going, and one morning sent for Pitou.

Now and then Pitou paid him a visit. Billet always welcomed him with open hand, made him take meals, if anything was on the board, or wine or cider, if it was the right time for drinks. But never had Billet sent for Pitou. Hence, it was not without disquiet that the young man proceeded to the farm.

Billet was always grave; nobody could say that he had seen a smile pass over his lips since his daughter had left the farm. This time he was graver than usual.

Still he held out his hand in the old manner to Pitou, shook his with more vigor than usual, and kept it in his, while the other looked at him with wonder.

"Pitou, you are an honest fellow," said the farmer.

"Faith, I believe I am," replied Pitou.

"I am sure of it."

"You are very good, Master Billet."

"It follows that, as I am going away, I shall leave you at the head of my farm."

"Impossible! There are a lot of petty matters for which a woman's eye is indispensable."

16

"I know it," replied Billet; "you can select the woman to share the superintendence with you. I shall not ask her name; I don't want to know it; and when I come down to the farm, I shall notify you a week ahead, so she will have time to get out of the way if she ought not to see me or I see her."

"Very well, Master Billet," said the new steward.

"Now, in the granary is the grain for sowing; also the hay and other fodder for the cattle, and in this drawer you see the cash to pay the hands." He opened a drawer full of hard money.

"Stop a bit, master. How much is in this drawer?"

"I do not know," rejoined Billet, locking the drawer and giving the key to Pitou, with the words; "When you want more, ask for it."

Pitou felt all the trust in this speech and put out his hand to grasp the other's, but was checked by his humility.

"Nonsense," said Billet; "why should not honest men grasp hands?"

"If you should want me in town?"

"Rest easy; I shall not forget you. It is two o'clock; I shall start for Paris at five. At six, you might be here with the woman you choose to second you."

"Right; but then, there is no time to lose," said Pitou. "I hope we shall soon meet again, dear Master Billet."

Billet watched him hurrying away as long as he could see him, and when he disappeared, he said: "Now, why did not Catherine fall in love with an honest chap like that, rather than one of those noble vermin who leaves her a mother without being a wife, and a widow without her being wed."

It is needless to say that Billet got upon the Villers Cotterets stage to ride to Paris at five, and that at six Catherine and little Isidore re-entered the farm.

Billet found himself among young men in the House, not merely representatives, but fighters; for it was felt that they had to wrestle with the unknown.

17

They were armed against two enemies, the clergy and the nobility. If these resisted, the orders were for them to be overcome.

The king was pitied, and the members were left free to treat him as occasion dictated. It was hoped that he might escape the threefold power of the queen, the clergy, and the aristocracy; if they upheld him, they would all be broken to pieces with him. They moved that the title of majesty should be suppressed.

"What shall we call the executive power, then?" asked a voice.

"Call him 'the King of the French,'" shouted Billet. "It is a pretty title enough for Capet to be satisfied with."

Moreover, instead of a throne, the King of the French had to content himself with a plain arm-chair, and that was placed on the left of the speaker's, so that the monarch should be subordinated.

In the absence of the king, the Constitution was sworn to by the sad, cold House, all aware that the impotent laws would not endure a year.

As these motions were equivalent to saying, "there is no longer a king." Money, as usual, took fright; down went the stocks dreadfully, and the bankers took alarm.

There was a revulsion in favor of the king, and his speech in the House was so applauded that he went to the theater that evening in high glee. That night he wrote to the powers of Europe that he had subscribed to the Constitution.

So far, the House had been tolerant, mild to the refractory priests, and paying pensions to the princes and nobles who had fled abroad.

We shall see how the nobles recompensed this mildness.

When they were debating on paying the old and infirm priests, though they might be opposed to the Reformation, news came from Avignon of a massacre of revolutionists by the religious fanatics, and a bloody reprisal of the other party.

As for the runaway nobles, still drawing revenue from their country, this is what they were doing.

They reconciled Austria with Prussia, making friends of two enemies. They induced Russia to forbid the French embassador going about the St. Petersburg streets, and sent a minister to the refugees at Coblentz. They made Berne punish a town for singing the "It shall go on." They led the kings to act roughly; Russia and Sweden sent back with unbroken seals Louis XVI.'s dispatches announcing his adhesion to the Constitution.

Spain refused to receive it, and a French revolutionist would have been burned by the Inquisition only for his committing suicide.

Venice threw on St. Mark's Place the corpse of a man strangled in the night by the Council of Ten, with the plain inscription: "This was a Freemason."

The Emperor and the King of Prussia did answer, but it was by a threat: "We trust we shall not have to take precautions against the repetition of events promising such sad auguries."

Hence there was a religious war in La Vendee and in the south, with prospective war abroad.

At present the intention of the crowned heads was to stifle the revolution rather than cut its throat.

The defiance of aristocratic Europe was accepted, and instead of waiting for the attack, the orator of the House cried for France to begin the movement.

The absentee princes were summoned home on penalty of losing all rights to the succession; the nobles' property was seized, unless they took the oath of allegiance to the country. The priests were granted a week to take the oath, or to be imprisoned, and no churches could be used for worship unless by the sworn clergy.

Lafayette's party wished the king to oppose his veto to these acts, but the queen so hated Lafayette that she induced the Court party to support Petion instead of the general for the post of mayor of Paris. Strange blindness, in favor of Petion, her rude jailer, who had brought her back from the flight to Varennes.

On the nineteenth of December the king vetoed the bill against the priests.

That night, at the Jacobin Club, the debate was hot. Virchaux, a Swiss, offered the society a sword for the first general who should vanquish the enemies of freedom. Isnard, the wrath of the House, a southerner, drew the sword, and leaped up into the rostrum, crying:

"Behold the sword of the exterminating angel! It will be victorious! France will give a loud call, and all the people will respond; the earth will then be covered with warriors, and the foes of liberty will be wiped out from the list of men!"

Ezekiel could not have spoken better. This drawn sword was not to be sheathed, for war broke out within and without. The Switzer's sword was first to smite the King of France, the foreign sovereigns afterward.

CHAPTER II. GILBERT'S CANDIDATE.

Dr. Gilbert had not seen the queen for six months, since he had let her know that he was informed by Cagliostro that she was deceiving him.

He was therefore astonished to see the king's valet enter his room one morning. He thought the king was sick and had sent for him, but the messenger reassured him. He was wanted in the palace, whither he hastened to go.

He was profoundly attached to the king; he pitied Marie Antoinette more as a woman than a queen. It was profound pity, for she inspired neither love nor devotion.

The lady waiting to greet Gilbert was the Princess Elizabeth. Neither king nor queen, after his showing them he saw they were playing him false, had dared to send directly to him; they put Lady Elizabeth forward.

Her first words proved to the doctor that he was not mistaken in his surmise.

"Doctor Gilbert," said she, "I do not know whether others have forgotten the tokens of interest you showed my brother on our return from Versailles, and those you showed my sister on our return from Varennes, but I remember."

"Madame," returned Gilbert, bowing, "God, in His wisdom, hath decided that you should have all the merits, memory included—a scarce virtue in our days, and particularly so among royal personages."

"I hope you are not referring to my brother, who often speaks of you, and praises your experience."

"As a medical adviser," remarked Gilbert, smiling.

"Yes; but he thinks you can be a physician to the realm as well as to the ruler."

"Very kind of the king. For which case is he calling me in at present?"

"It is not the king who calls you, sir, but I," responded the lady, blushing; for her chaste heart knew not how to lie.

"You? Your health worries me the least; your pallor arises from fatigue and disquiet, not from bad health."

"You are right; I am not trembling for myself, but my brother, who makes me fret."

"So he does me, madame."

"Oh, our uneasiness does not probably spring from the same cause, as I am concerned about his health. I do not mean that he is unwell, but he is downcast and disheartened. Some ten days ago—I am counting the days now—he ceased speaking, except to me, and in his favorite pastime of backgammon he only utters the necessary terms of the game."

"It is eleven days since he went to the House to present his veto. Why was he not mute that day instead of the next?"

"Is it your opinion that he should have sanctioned that impious decree?" demanded the princess, quickly.

"My opinion is, that to put the king in front of the priests in the coming tide, the rising storm, is to have priests and king broken by the same wave."

"What would you do in my poor brother's place, doctor?"

"A party is growing, like those genii of the Arabian Nights, which becomes a hundred cubits high an hour after release from the imprisoning bottle."

"You allude to the Jacobins?"

Gilbert shook his head.

"No; I mean the Girondists, who wish for war, a national desire."

"But war with whom? With the emperor, our brother? The King of

Spain, our nephew? Our enemies, Doctor Gilbert, are at home, and not outside of France, in proof of which—" She hesitated, but he besought her to speak.

"I really do not know that I can tell you, though it is the reason of my asking you here."

"You may speak freely to one who is devoted and ready to give his life to the king."

"Do you believe there is any counterbane?" she inquired.

"Universal?" queried Gilbert, smiling. "No, madame; each venomous substance has its antidote, though they are of little avail generally."

"What a pity!"

"There are two kinds of poisons, mineral and vegetable—of what sort would you speak?"

"Doctor, I am going to tell you a great secret. One of our cooks, who left the royal kitchen to set up a bakery of his own, has returned to our service, with the intention of murdering the king. This red-hot Jacobin has been heard crying that France would be relieved if the king were put out of the way."

"In general, men fit for such a crime do not go about bragging beforehand. But I suppose you take precautions?"

"Yes; it is settled that the king shall live on roast meat, with a trusty hand to supply the bread and wine. As the king is fond of pastry, Madame Campan orders what he likes, as though for herself. We are warned especially against powdered sugar."

"In which arsenic might be mixed unnoticed?"

"Exactly. It was the queen's habit to use it for her lemonade, but we have entirely given up the use of it. The king, the queen, and I take meals together, ringing for what we want. Madame Campan brings us what we like, secretly, and hides it under the table; we pretend to eat the usual things while the servants are in the room. This is how we live, sir; and yet the queen and I tremble every instant lest the king should turn pale and cry out he was in pain."

"Let me say at once, madame," returned the doctor, "that I do not believe in these threats of poisoning; but in any event, I am under his majesty's orders. What does the king desire? That I should have lodgings in the palace? I will stay here in such a way as to be at hand until the fears are over."

"Oh, my brother is not afraid!" the princess hastened to say.

"I did not mean that. Until your fears are over. I have some practice in poisonings and their remedies. I am ready to baffle them in whatever shape they are presented; but allow me to say, madame, that all fears for the king might be removed if he were willing."

"Oh, what must be done for that?" intervened a voice, not the Lady Elizabeth's, and which, by its emphatic and ringing tone, made Gilbert turn.

It was the queen, and he bowed.

"Has the queen doubted the sincerity of my offers?"

"Oh, sir, so many heads and hearts have turned in this tempestuous wind, that one knows not whom to trust."

"Which is why your majesty receives from the Feuillants Club a Premier shaped by the Baroness de Stael?"

"You know that?" cried the royal lady, starting.

"I know your majesty is pledged to take Count Louis de Narbonne."

"And, of course, you blame me?"

"No; it is a trial like others. When the king shall have tried all, he may finish by the one with whom he should have commenced."

"You know Madame de Stael? What do you think of her?"

"Physically, she is not altogether attractive."

The queen smiled; as a woman, she was not sorry to hear another woman decried who just then was widely talked about.

"But her talent, her parts, her merits?"

"She is good and generous, madame; none of her enemies would remain so after a quarter of an hour's conversation."

"I speak of her genius, sir; politics are not managed by the heart."

"Madame, the heart spoils nothing, not even in politics; but let us not use the word genius rashly. Madame de Stael has great and immense talent, but it does not rise to genius; she is as iron to the steel of her master, Rousseau. As a politician, she is given more heed than she deserves. Her drawing-room is the meeting-place of the English party. Coming of the middle class as she does, and that the money-worshiping middle class, she has the weakness of loving a lord; she admires the English from thinking that they are an aristocratic people. Being ignorant of the history of England, and the mechanism of its government, she takes for the descendants of the Norman Conquerors the baronets created yesterday. With old material, other people make a new stock; with the new, England often makes the old."

"Do you see in this why Baroness de Stael proposes De Narbonne to us?"

"Hem! This time, madame, two likings are combined: that for the aristocracy and the aristocrat."

"Do you imagine that she loves Louis de Narbonne on account of his descent?"

(Louis de Narbonne was supposed to be an incestuous son of King Louis XV.)

"It is not on account of any ability, I reckon?"

"But nobody is less well-born than Louis de Narbonne; his father is not even known."

"Only because one dares not look at the sun."

"So you do not believe that De Narbonne is the outcome of the Swedish Embassy, as the Jacobins assert, with Robespierre at the head?"

"Yes; only he comes from the wife's boudoir, not the lord's study. To suppose Lord de Stael has a hand in it, is to suppose he is master in his own house. Goodness, no; this is not an embassador's treachery, but a loving woman's weakness. Nothing but Love, the great, eternal magician, could impel a woman to put the gigantic sword of the revolution in that frivolous rake's hands."

"Do you allude to the demagogue Isnard kissed at the Jacobin Club?"

"Alas, madame, I speak of the one suspended over your head."

"Therefore, it is your opinion that we are wrong to accept De Narbonne as Minister of War?"

"You would do better to take at once his successor, Dumouriez."

"A soldier of fortune?"

"Ha! the worst word is spoken; and it is unfair any way."

"Was not Dumouriez a private soldier?"

"I am well aware that Dumouriez is not of that court nobility to which everything is sacrificed. Of the rustic nobility, unable to obtain a rank, he enlisted as a common soldier. At twenty years he fought five or six troopers, though hacked badly, and despite this proof of courage, he languished in the ranks."

"He sharpened his wits by serving Louis XV. as spy."

"Why do you call that spying in him which you rate diplomacy in others? I know that he carried on correspondence with the king without the knowledge of the ministers; but what noble of the court does not do the same?"

"But, doctor, this man whom you recommend is essentially a most immoral one," exclaimed the queen, betraying her deep knowledge of politics by the details into which she went. "He has no principles—no idea of honor. The Duke of Choiseul told me that he laid before him two plans about Corsica—one to set her free, the other to subdue her."

"Quite true; but Choiseul failed to say that the former was preferred, and that Dumouriez fought bravely for its success."

"The day when we accept him for minister it will be equivalent to a declaration of war to all Europe."

"Why, madame, this declaration is already made in all hearts," retorted Gilbert. "Do you know how many names are down in this district as volunteers to start for the campaign? Six hundred thousand. In the Jura, the women have proposed all the men shall march, as they, with pikes, will guard their homes."

"You have spoken a word which makes me shudder—pikes! Oh, the pikes of '89! I can ever see the heads of my Life Guardsmen carried on the pikes' point."

"Nevertheless, it was a woman, a mother, who suggested a national subscription to manufacture pikes."

"Was it also a woman who suggested your Jacobins adopting the red cap of liberty, the color of blood?"

"Your majesty is in error on that point," said Gilbert, although he did not care to enlighten the queen wholly on the ancient head-gear. "A symbol was wanted of equality, and as all Frenchmen could not well dress alike, a part of a dress was alone adopted: the cap such as the poor peasant wears. The red color was preferred, not as it happens to be that of blood, but because gay, bright, and a favorite with the masses."

"All very fine, doctor," sneered the queen. "I do not despair of seeing such a partisan of novelties coming some day to feel the king's pulse, with the red cap on your head and a pike in your hand."

Seeing that she could not win with such a man, the queen retired, half jesting, half bitter.

Princess Elizabeth was about to do the same, when Gilbert appealed to her:

"You love your brother, do you not?"

"Love? The feeling is of adoration."

"Then you are ready to transmit good advice to him, coming from a friend?"

"Then, speak, speak!"

"When his Feuillant Ministry falls, which will not take long, let him take a ministry with all the members wearing this red cap, though it so alarms the queen." And profoundly bowing, he went out.

CHAPTER III. POWERFUL, PERHAPS; HAPPY, NEVER.

The Narbonne Ministry lasted three months. A speech of Vergniaud blasted it. On the news that the Empress of Russia had made a treaty with Turkey, and Austria and Prussia had signed an alliance, offensive and defensive, he sprung into the rostrum and cried:

"I see the palace from here where this counter-revolution is scheming those plots which aim to deliver us to Austria. The day has come when you must put an end to so much audacity, and confound the plotters. Out of that palace have issued panic and terror in olden times, in the name of despotism—let them now rush into it in the name of the law!"

Dread and terror did indeed enter the Tuileries, whence De Narbonne, wafted thither by a breath of love, was expelled by a gust of storm. This downfall occurred at the beginning of March, 1792.

Scarce three months after the interview of Gilbert and the queen, a small, active, nervy little man, with flaming eyes blazing in a bright face, was ushered into King Louis' presence. He was aged fifty-six, but appeared ten years younger, though his cheek was brown with camp-fire smoke; he wore the uniform of a camp-marshal.

The king cast a dull and heavy glance on the little man, whom he had never met; but it was not without observation. The other fixed on him a scrutinizing eye full of fire and distrust.

"You are General Dumouriez? Count de Narbonne, I believe, called you to Paris?"

"To announce that he gave me a division in the army in Alsace."

"But you did not join, it appears?"

"Sire, I accepted; but I felt that I ought to point out that as war impended"—Louis started visibly—"and threatened to become general," went on the soldier, without appearing to remark the emotion, "I deemed it good to occupy the south, where an attack might come unawares; consequently, it seemed urgent to me that a plan for movements there should be drawn up, and a general and army sent thither."

"Yes; and you gave this plan to Count de Narbonne, after showing it to members of the Gironde?"

"They are friends of mine, as I believe they are of your majesty."

"Then I am dealing with a Girondist?" queried the monarch, smiling.

"With a patriot, and faithful subject of his king."

Louis bit his thick lips.

"Was it to serve the king and the country the more efficaciously that you refused to be foreign minister for a time?"

"Sire, I replied that I preferred, to being any kind of minister, the command promised me. I am a soldier, not a statesman."

"I have been assured, on the contrary, that you are both," observed the sovereign.

"I am praised too highly, sire."

"It was on that assurance that I insisted."

"Yes, sire; but in spite of my great regret, I was obliged to persist in refusing."

"Why refuse?"

"Because it is a crisis. It has upset De Narbonne and compromises Lessart. Any man has the right to keep out of employment or be employed, according to what he thinks he is fitted for. Now, my liege, I am good for something or for nothing. If the latter, leave me in my obscurity. Who knows for what fate you draw me forth? If I am good for something, do not give me power for an instant, the premier of a day, but place some solid footing under me that I may be your support at another day. Our affairs—your majesty will pardon me already regarding his business as mine—our affairs are in too great disfavor abroad for courts to deal with an ad interim ministry; this interregnum—you will excuse the frankness of an old soldier"—no one was less frank than Dumouriez, but he wanted to appear so at times—"this interval will be a blunder against which the House will revolt, and it will make me disliked there; more, I must say that it will injure the king, who will seem still to cling to his former Cabinet, and only be waiting for a chance to bring it back."

"Were that my intention, do you not believe it possible, sir?"

"I believe, sire, that it is full time to drop the past."

"And make myself a Jacobin, as you have said to my valet, Laporte?"

"Forsooth, did your majesty this, it would perplex all the parties, and the Jacobins most of all."

"Why not straightway advise me to don the red cap?"

"I wish I saw you in it," said Dumouriez.

For an instant the king eyed with distrust the man who had thus replied to him; and then he resumed:

"So you want a permanent office?"

"I am wishing nothing at all, only ready to receive the king's orders; still, I should prefer them to send me to the frontier to retaining me in town."

"But if I give you the order to stay, and the foreign office portfolio in permanency, what will you say?"

"That your majesty has dispelled your prejudices against me," returned the general, with a smile.

"Well, yes, entirely, general; you are my premier."

"Sire, I am devoted to your service; but—"

"Restrictions?"

"Explanations, sire. The first minister's place is not what it was. Without ceasing to be your majesty's faithful servant on entering the post, I become the man of the nation. From this day, do not expect the language my predecessors used; I must speak according to the Constitution and liberty. Confined to my duties, I shall not play the courtier; I shall not have the time, and I drop all etiquette so as to better serve the king. I shall only work with you in private or at the council—and I warn you that it will be hard work."

"Hard work—why?"

"Why, it is plain; almost all your diplomatic corps are anti-revolutionists. I must urge you to change them, cross your tastes on the new choice, propose officials of whom your majesty never so much as heard the names, and others who will displease."

"In which case?" quickly interrupted Louis.

"Then I shall obey when your majesty's repugnance is too strong and well-founded, as you are the master; but if your choice is suggested by your surroundings, and is clearly made to get me into trouble, I shall entreat your majesty to find a successor for me. Sire, think of the dreadful dangers besieging your throne, and that one must have the public confidence in support; sire, this depends on you."

"Let me stay you a moment; I have long pondered over these dangers." He stretched out his hand to the portrait of Charles I. of England, by Vandyke, and continued, while wiping his forehead with his handkerchief: "This would remind me, if I were to forget them. It is the same situation, with similar dangers; perhaps the scaffold of Whitehall is erecting on City Hall Place."

"You are looking too far ahead, my lord."

"Only to the horizon. In this event, I shall march to the scaffold as Charles I. did, not perhaps as knightly, but at least as like a Christian. Proceed, general."

Dumouriez was checked by this firmness, which he had not expected.

"Sire, allow me to change the subject."

"As you like; I only wish to show that I am not daunted by the prospect they try to frighten me with, but that I am prepared for even this emergency."

"If I am still regarded as your Minister of Foreign Affairs, I will bring four dispatches to the first consul. I notify your majesty that they will not resemble those of previous issue in style or principles; they will suit the circumstances. If this first piece of work suits your majesty, I will continue; if not, my carriage will be waiting to carry me to serve king and country on the border; and, whatever may be said about my diplomatic ability," added Dumouriez, "war is my true element, and the object of my labors these thirty-six years."

"Wait," said the other, as he bowed before going out; "we agree on one point, but there are six more to settle."

"My colleagues?"

"Yes; I do not want you to say that you are hampered by such a one. Choose your Cabinet, sir."

"Sire, you are fixing grave responsibility on me."

"I believe I am meeting your wishes by putting it on you."

"Sire, I know nobody at Paris save one, Lacoste, whom I propose for the navy office."

"Lacoste? A clerk in the naval stores, I believe?" questioned the king.

"Who resigned rather than connive at some foul play."

"That's a good recommendation. What about the others?'"

"I must consult Petion, Brissot, Condorcet—"

"The Girondists, in short?"

"Yes, sire."

"Let the Gironde pass; we shall see if they will get us out of the ditch better than the other parties."

"We have still to learn if the four dispatches will suit."

"We might learn that this evening; we can hold an extraordinary council, composed of yourself, Grave, and Gerville—Duport has resigned. But do not go yet; I want to commit you."

He had hardly spoken before the queen and Princess Elizabeth stood in the room, holding prayer-books.

"Ladies," said the king, "this is General Dumouriez, who promises to serve us well, and will arrange a new Cabinet with us this evening."

Dumouriez bowed, while the queen looked hard at the little man who was to exercise so much influence over the affairs of France.

"Do you know Doctor Gilbert?" she asked. "If not, make his acquaintance as an excellent prophet. Three months ago he foretold that you would be Count de Narbonne's successor."

The main doors opened, for the king was going to mass. Behind him Dumouriez went out; but the courtiers shunned him as though he had the leprosy.

"I told you I should get you committed," whispered the monarch.

"Committed to you, but not to the aristocracy," returned the warrior; "it is a fresh favor the king grants me." Whereupon he retired.

At the appointed hour he returned with the four dispatches promised— for Spain, Prussia, England, and Austria. He read them to the king and Messieurs Grave and Gerville, but he guessed that he had another auditor behind the tapestry by its shaking.

The new ruler spoke in the king's name, but in the sense of the Constitution, without threats, but also without weakness. He discussed the true interests of each power relatively to the French Revolution. As each had complained of the Jacobin pamphlets, he ascribed the despicable insults to the freedom of the press, a sun which made weeds to grow as well as good grain to flourish. Lastly, he demanded peace in the name of a free nation, of which the king was the hereditary representative.

The listening king lent fresh interest to each paper.

"I never heard the like, general," he said, when the reading was over.

"That is how ministers should speak and write in the name of rulers," observed Gerville.

"Well, give me the papers; they shall go off to-morrow," the king said.

"Sire, the messengers are waiting in the palace yard," said Dumouriez.

"I wanted to have a duplicate made to show the queen," objected the king, with marked hesitation.

"I foresaw the wish, and have copies here," replied Dumouriez.

"Send off the dispatches," rejoined the king.

The general took them to the door, behind which an aid was waiting. Immediately the gallop of several horses was heard leaving the Tuileries together.

"Be it so," said the king, replying to his mind, as the meaning sounds died away. "Now, about your Cabinet?"

"Monsieur Gerville pleads that his health will not allow him to remain, and Monsieur Grave, stung by a criticism of Madame Roland, wishes to hold office until his successor is found. I therefore pray your majesty to receive Colonel Servan, an honest man in the full acceptation of the words, of a solid material, pure manners, philosophical austerity, and a heart like a woman's, withal an enlightened patriot, a courageous soldier, and a vigilant statesman."

"Colonel Servan is taken. So we have three ministers: Dumouriez for the Foreign Office, Servan for War, and Lacoste for the Navy. Who shall be in the Treasury?"

"Clavieres, if you will. He is a man with great financial friends and supreme skill in handling money."

"Be it so. As for the Law lord?"

"A lawyer of Bordeaux has been recommended to me—Duranthon."

"Belonging to the Gironde party, of course?"

"Yes, sire, but enlightened, upright, a very good citizen, though slow and feeble; we will infuse fire into him and be strong enough for all of us."

"The Home Department remains."

"The general opinion is that this will be fitted to Roland."

"You mean Madame Roland?"

"To the Roland couple. I do not know them, but I am assured that the one resembles a character of Plutarch and the other a woman from Livy."

"Do you know that your Cabinet is already called the Breechless Ministry?"

"I accept the nickname, with the hope that it will be found without breaches."

"We will hold the council with them the day after to-morrow."

General Dumouriez was going away with his colleagues, when a valet called him aside and said that the king had something more to say to him.

"The king or the queen?" he questioned.

"It is the queen, sir; but she thought there was no need for those gentlemen to know that."

And Weber—for this was the Austrian foster-brother of Marie Antoinette—conducted the general to the queen's apartments, where he introduced him as the person sent for.

Dumouriez entered, with his heart beating more violently than when he led a charge or mounted the deadly breach. He fully understood that he had never stood in worse danger. The road he traveled was strewn with corpses, and he might stumble over the dead reputations of premiers, from Calonne to Lafayette.

The queen was walking up and down, with a very red face. She advanced with a majestic and irritated air as he stopped on the sill where the door had been closed behind him.

"Sir, you are all-powerful at this juncture," she said, breaking the ice with her customary vivacity. "But it is by favor of the populace, who soon shatter their idols. You are said to have much talent. Have the wit, to begin with, to understand that the king and I will not suffer novelties. Your constitution is a pneumatic machine; royalty stifles in it for want of air. So I have sent for you to learn, before you go further, whether you side with us or with the Jacobins."

"Madame," responded Dumouriez, "I am pained by this confidence, although I expected it, from the impression that your majesty was behind the tapestry."

"Which means that you have your reply ready?"

"It is that I stand between king and country, but before all I belong to the country."

"The country?" sneered the queen. "Is the king no longer anything, that everybody belongs to the country and none to him?"

"Excuse me, lady; the king is always the king, but he has taken oath to the Constitution, and from that day he should be one of the first slaves of the Constitution."

"A compulsory oath, and in no way binding, sir!"

Dumouriez held his tongue for a space, and, being a consummate actor, he regarded the speaker with deep pity.

"Madame," he said, at length, "allow me to say that your safety, the king's, your children's, all, are attached to this Constitution which you deride, and which will save you, if you consent to be saved by it. I should serve you badly, as well as the king, if I spoke otherwise to you."

The queen interrupted him with an imperious gesture.

"Oh, sir, sir, I assure you that you are on the wrong path!" she said; adding, with an indescribable accent of threat: "Take heed for yourself!"

"Madame," replied Dumouriez, in a perfectly calm tone, "I am over fifty years of age; my life has been traversed with perils, and on taking the ministry I said to myself that ministerial responsibility was not the slightest danger I ever ran."

"Fy, sir!" returned the queen, slapping her hands together; "you have nothing more to do than to slander me?"

"Slander you, madame?"

"Yes; do you want me to explain the meaning of the words I used? It is that I am capable of having you assassinated. For shame, sir!"

Tears escaped from her eyes. Dumouriez had gone as far as she wanted; he knew that some sensitive fiber remained in that indurated heart.

"Lord forbid I should so insult my queen!" he cried. "The nature of your majesty is too grand and noble for the worst of her enemies to be inspired with such an idea, she has given heroic proofs which I have admired, and which attached me to her."

"Then excuse me, and lend me your arm. I am so weak that I often fear I shall fall in a swoon."

Turning pale, she indeed drooped her head backward. Was it reality, or only one of the wiles in which this fearful Medea was so skilled? Keen though the general was, he was deceived; or else, more cunning than the enchantress, he feigned to be caught.

"Believe me, madame," he said, "that I have no interest in cheating you. I abhor anarchy and crime as much as yourself. Believe, too, that I have experience, and am better placed than your majesty to see events. What is transpiring is not an intrigue of the Duke of Orleans, as you are led to think; not the effect of Pitt's hatred, as you have supposed; not even the outcome of popular impulse, but the almost unanimous insurrection of a great nation against inveterate abuses. I grant that there is in all this great hates which fan the flames. Leave the lunatics and the villains on one side; let us see nothing in this revolution in progress but the king and the nation, all tending to separate them brings about their mutual ruin. I come, my lady, to work my utmost to reunite them; aid me, instead of thwarting me. You mistrust me? Am I an obstacle to your anti-revolutionary projects? Tell me so, madame, I will forthwith hand my resignation to the king, and go and wail the fate of my country and its ruler in some nook."

"No, no," said the queen; "remain, and excuse me."

"Do you ask me to excuse you? Oh, madame, I entreat you not to humble yourself thus."

"Why should I not be humble? Am I still a queen? am I yet treated like a woman?"

Going to the window, she opened it in spite of the evening coolness; the moon silvered the leafless trees of the palace gardens.

"Are not the air and the sunshine free to all? Well, these are refused to me; I dare not put my head out of window, either on the street or the gardens. Yesterday I did look out on the yard, when a Guards gunner hailed me with an insulting nickname, and said: 'How I should like to carry your head on a bayonet-point.' This morning, I opened the garden window. A man standing on a chair was reading infamous stuff against me; a priest was dragged to a fountain to be ducked; and meanwhile, as though such scenes were matters of course, children were sailing their balloons and couples were strolling tranquilly. What times we are living in—what a place to live in—what a people! And would you have me still believe myself a queen, and even feel like a woman?"

She threw herself on a sofa, and hid her face in her hands.

Dumouriez dropped on one knee, and taking up the hem of her dress respectfully, he kissed it.

"Lady," he said, "from the time when I undertake this struggle, you will become the mighty queen and the happy woman once more, or I shall leave my life on the battle-field."

Rising, he saluted the lady and hurried out. She watched him go with a hopeless look, repeating:

"The mighty queen? Perhaps, thanks to your sword—for it is possible; but the happy woman—never, never, never!"

She let her head fall between the sofa cushions, muttering the name dearer every day and more painful:

"Charny!"

The Dumouriez Cabinet might be called one of war.

On the first of March, the Emperor Leopold died in the midst of his Italian harem, slain by self-compounded aphrodisiacs. The queen, who had read in some lampoon that a penny pie would settle the monarchy, and who had called Dr. Gilbert in to get an antidote, cried aloud that her brother was poisoned. With him passed all the halting policy of Austria.

Francis II., who mounted the throne, was of mixed Italian and German blood. An Austrian born at Florence, he was weak, violent, and tricky. The priests reckoned him an honest man; his hard and bigoted soul hid its duplicity under a rosy face of dreadful sameness. He walked like a stage ghost; he gave his daughter to a conqueror rather than part with his estate, and then stabbed him in the back at his first retreating step in the snows. Francis II. remains in history the tyrant of the Leads of Venice and the Spitzberg dungeons, and the torturer of Andryane and Silvio Pellico.

This was the protector of the French fugitives, the ally of Prussia and the enemy of France. He held Embassador Noailles as a prisoner at Vienna.

The French embassador to Berlin, Segur, was preceded by a rumor that he expected to gain the secrets of the King of Prussia by making love to his mistresses—this King of Prussia was a lady-killer! Segur presented himself at the same time as the envoy from the self-exiled princes at Coblentz.

The king turned his back on the French representative, and asked pointedly after the health of the Prince of Artois.

These were the two ostensible foes; the hidden ones were Spain, Russia, and England. The chief of the coalition was to be the King of Sweden, that dwarf in giant's armor whom Catherine II. held up in her hand.

With the ascension of Francis, the diplomatic note came: Austria was to rule in France, Avignon was to be restored to the pope, and things in France were to go back to where they stood in June, 1789.

This note evidently agreed with the secret wishes of the king and the queen. Dumouriez laughed at it. But he took it to the king.

As much as Marie Antoinette, the woman for extreme measures, desired a war which she believed one of deliverance for her, the king feared it, as the man for the medium, slowness, wavering, and crooked policy. Indeed, suppose a victory in the war, he would be at the mercy of the victorious general; suppose a defeat, and the people would hold him responsible, cry treason, and rush on the palace!

In short, should the enemy penetrate to Paris, what would it bring? The king's brother, Count Provence, who aimed to be regent of the realm. The result of the return of the runaway princes would be the king deposed, Marie Antoinette pronounced an adulteress, and the royal children proclaimed, perhaps, illegitimate.

The king trusted foreigners, but not the princes of his own blood and kingdom.

On reading the note, he comprehended that the hour to draw the sword for France had come, and that there was no receding.

Who was to bear the flag of the revolution? Lafayette, who had lost his fame by massacring the populace on the Paris parade-ground; Luckner, who was known only by the mischief he wrought in the Seven Years' War, and old Rochambeau, the French naval hero in the American Revolution, who was for defensive war, and was vexed to see Dumouriez promote young blood over his head without benefiting by his experience.

It was expected that Lafayette would be victorious in the north; when he would be commander-in-chief, Dumouriez would be the Minister of War; they would cast down the red cap and crush Jacobins and Girondists with the two hands.

The counter-revolution was ready.

But what were Robespierre and the Invisibles doing—that great secret society which held the agitators in its grasp as Jove holds the writhing thunderbolts? Robespierre was in the shade, and many asserted that he was bribed by the royal family.

At the outset all went well for the Royalists; Lafayette's lieutenants, two Royalists, Dillon and Biron, headed a rout before Lille; the scouts, dragoons, still the most aristocratic arm of the service, turned tail and started a panic. The runaways accused the captains of treachery, and murdered Dillon and other officers. The Gironde accused the queen and Court party of organizing the flight.

The popular clamor compelled Marie Antoinette to let the Constitutional Guard be abolished—another name for a royal life-guard—and it was superseded by the Paris National Guards.

Oh! Charny, Charny, where were you?—you who, at Varennes, nearly rescued the queen with but three hundred horsemen—what would you not have done at Paris with six thousand desperadoes?

Charny was happy, forgetting everything in the arms of his countess.

CHAPTER IV. THE FOES FACE TO FACE.

While the queen was looking from the palace to see the Austrians coming, another was watching in her little reception-rooms. One was revolution embodied, the other its opponents intensified; that was Madame Roland, this the queen from Austria.

The real war at this period was between this pair.

A singular thing, both had such influence over their husbands as to lead them to death, although by different roads.

Dumouriez had thrown a sop to the Jacobins without knowing who the Colonel Servan was whom he took for Minister of War. He was a favorite of Madame Roland. Like all the Girondists, of whom she was the light, the fire, the egeria, he was inspired by that valiant spirit.

But he and Roland were neutralized at the council by Dumouriez. They had forced the Royalist Constitutional Guards to disband, but they had merely changed their uniform for that of the Swiss Guards, the sworn defenders of royalty, and swaggered about the streets more insolently than before.

Madame Roland suggested that, on the occasion of the July festivals, a camp of twenty thousand volunteers should be established in Paris. Servan was to present this as a citizen, apart from his being a minister. In the same way, Roland was to punish the rebellious priests who were preaching from the pulpits that taxpayers would be damned, by ordering their exile.

Dumouriez supported the volunteer proposition at the council, in the hope that the new-comers would be Jacobins; that is, the Invisibles, by whom neither the Girondists nor the Feuillants would profit.

"If your majesty vetoes it," he said, firmly, "instead of the twenty thousand authorized, we shall have forty thousand unruly spirits in town, who may with one rush upset Constitution, Assembly, and the throne. Had we been vanquishers—But we must give in—I say accept."

But the queen urged the king to stand firm. As we know, she would rather be lost than be saved by Lafayette.

As for the decree against the priests, it was another matter. The king said that he wavered in temporal questions as he judged them with his mind, which was fallible; but he tried religious matters with his conscience, which was infallible!

But they could not dispense with Dumouriez at this juncture.

"Accept the volunteer act," said the queen, at last; "let the camp be at Soissons, where the general says he will gradually draft them off out of the way; and—well, we will see about the decree aimed at the priests. Dumouriez has your promise, but there must be some way of evading the issue when you are the Jesuits' pupil!"

Roland, Servan, and Clavieres resigned, and the Assembly applauded their act as deserving the thanks of the country.

Hearing of this, and that Dumouriez was badly compromised, the pupil of Vauguyon agreed to the Volunteer Camp Bill, but pleading conscientious scruples, deferred signing the decree banishing the refractory priests. This made the new ministers wince, and Dumouriez went away sore at heart. The king had almost succeeded in baffling him, the fine diplomatist, sharp politician, and the general whose courage was doubled by intrigue!

He found at home the spies' reports that the Invisibles were holding meetings in the working quarters, and openly at Santerre's brewery. He wrote to warn the king, whose answer was:

"Do not believe that I can be bullied; my mind is made up."

Dumouriez replied, asking for an audience, and requested his successor to be sought for. It was clear that the anti-revolutionist party felt strong.

Indeed, they were reckoning on the following forces:

The Constitutional Guards, six thousand strong, disbanded, but ready to fly to arms at the first call; seven or eight thousand Knights of the Order of St. Louis, whose red ribbon was the rallying token; three battalions of Switzers, sixteen hundred men, picked soldiers, unshaken as the old Helvetic rocks.

Better than all, Lafayette had written: "Persist, sire; fortified with the authority the National Assembly has delegated to you, you will find all good citizens on your side!"

The plan was to gather all the forces at a given signal, seize the cannon of each section of Paris, shut up the Jacobin's Club-house and the Assembly, add all the Royalists in the National Guard, say, a contingent of fifteen thousand men, and wait for Lafayette, who might march up in three days.

The misfortune was that the queen would not hear of Lafayette. Lafayette was merely the Revolution moderated, and might prolong it and lead to a republic like that he had brought round in America; while the Jacobins' outrageous rule would sicken the people and could not endure.

Oh, had Charny been at hand! But it was not even known where he was; and were it known, it would be too low an abasement for the woman, if not the queen, to have recourse to him.

The night passed tumultuously at the palace, where they had the means of defense and attack, but not a hand strong enough to grasp and hurl them.

Dumouriez and his colleagues came to resign. They affirmed they were willing to die for the king, but to do this for the clergy would only precipitate the downfall of the monarchy.

"Sire," pleaded Dumouriez, "your conscience is misled; you are beguiled into civil war. Without strength, you must succumb, and history, while sorrowing for you, will blame you for causing the woes of France."

"Heaven be my witness that I wished but her happiness!"

"I do not doubt that; but one must account to the King of kings not only for purity of intentions, but the enlightened use of intentions. You suppose you are saving religion, but you will destroy it; your priests will be massacred; your broken crown will roll in your blood, the queen's, your children's, perhaps—oh, my king, my king!"

Choking, he applied his lips to the royal hand. With perfect serenity, and a majesty of which he might not be believed capable, Louis replied.

"You are right, general. I expect death, and forgive my murderers beforehand. You have well served me; I esteem you, and am affected by your sympathy. Farewell, sir!"

With Dumouriez going, royalty had parted with its last stay. The king threw off the mask, and stood with uncovered face before the people.

Let us see what the people were doing on their side.

CHAPTER V. THE UNINVITED VISITORS.

All day long a man in general's uniform was riding about the St. Antoine suburb, on a large Flanders horse, shaking hands right and left, kissing the girls and treating the men to drink. This was one of Lafayette's half dozen heirs, the small-change of the commander of the National Guard—Battalion Commander Santerre.

Beside him rode, on a fiery charger, like an aid next his general, a stout man who might by his dress be taken to be a well-to-do farmer. A scar tracked his brow, and he had as gloomy an eye and scowling a face as the battalion commander had an open countenance and frank smile.

"Get ready, my good friends; watch over the nation, against which traitors are plotting. But we are on guard," Santerre kept saying.

"What are we to do, friend Santerre?" asked the working-men. "You know that we are all your own. Where are the traitors? Lead us at them!"

"Wait; the proper time has not come."

"When will it strike?"

Santerre did not know a word about it; so he replied at a hazard, "Keep ready; we'll let you know."

But the man who rode by his knee, bending down over the horse's neck, would make signs to some men, and whisper:

"June twenty."

Whereupon these men would call groups of twenty or so around each, and repeat the date to them, so that it would be circulated. Nobody knew what would be done on the twentieth of June, but all felt sure that something would happen on that day.

By whom was this mob moved, stirred, and excited? By a man of powerful build, leonine mane, and roaring voice, whom Santerre was to find waiting in his brewery office—Danton.

None better than this terrible wizard of the Revolution could evoke terror from the slums and hurl it into the old palace of Catherine di Medicis. Danton was the gong of riots; the blow he received he imparted vibratingly to all the multitude around him. Through Hebert he was linked to the populace, as by the Duke of Orleans he was affixed to the throne.

Whence came his power, doomed to be so fatal to royalty? To the queen, the spiteful Austrian who had not liked Lafayette to be mayor of Paris, but preferred Petion, the Republican, who had no sooner brought back the fugitive king to the Tuileries than he set to watch him closely.

Petion had made his two friends, Manuel and Danton, the Public Prosecutor and the Vice, respectively.

On the twentieth of June, under the pretext of presenting a petition to the king and raising a liberty pole, the palace was to be stormed.

The adepts alone knew that France was to be saved from the Lafayettes and the Moderates, and a warning to be given to the incorrigible monarch that there are some political tempests in which a vessel may be swamped with all hands aboard; that is, a king be overwhelmed with throne and family as in the oceanic abysses.

Billet knew more than Santerre when he accompanied him on his tour, after presenting himself as from the committee.

Danton called on the brewer to arrange for the meeting of the popular leaders that night at Charenton for the march on the morrow, presumably to the House, but really to the Tuileries.

The watchword was, "Have done with the palace!" but the way remained vague.

On the evening of the nineteenth, the queen saw a woman clad in scarlet, with a belt full of pistols, gallop, bold and terrible, along the main streets. It was Theroigne Mericourt, the beauty of Liege, who had gone back to her native country to help its rebellion; but the Austrians had caught her and kept her imprisoned for eighteen months.

She returned mysteriously to be at the bloody feast of the coming day. The courtesan of opulence, she was now the beloved of the people; from her noble lovers had come the funds for her costly weapons, which were not all for show. Hence the mob hailed her with cheers.

From the Tuileries garret, where the queen had climbed on hearing the uproar, she saw tables set out in the public squares and wine broached; patriotic songs were sung and at every toast fists were shaken at the palace.

Who were the guests? The Federals of Marseilles, led by Barbaroux, who brought with them the song worth an army—"the Marseillaise Hymn of Liberty."

Day breaks early in June. At five o'clock the battalions were marshaled, for the insurrection was regularized by this time and had a military aspect. The mob had chiefs, submitted to discipline, and fell into assigned places under flags.

Santerre was on horseback, with his staff of men from the working district. Billet did not leave him, for the occult power of the Invisibles charged him to watch over him.

Of the three corps into which the forces were divided, Santerre commanded the first, St. Huruge the second, and Theroigne the last.

About eleven, on an order brought by an unknown man, the immense mass started out. It numbered some twenty thousand when it left the Bastile Square.

It had a wild, odd, and horrible look.

Santerre's battalion was the most regular, having many in uniform, and muskets and bayonets among the weapons. But the other two were armed mobs, haggard, thin, and in rags from three years of revolutions and four of famine.

Neither had uniforms nor muskets, but tattered coats and smocks;

quaint arms snatched up in the first impulse of self-defense and anger: pikes, cooking-spits, jagged spears, hiltless swords, knives lashed to long poles, broad-axes, stone-masons' hammers and curriers' knives.

For standards, a gallows with a dangling doll, meant for the queen; a bull's head, with an obscene card stuck on the horns; a calf's heart on a spit, with the motto: "An Aristocrat's;" while flags showed the legends: "Sanction the decrees, or death!"—"Recall the patriotic ministers!"—"Tremble, tyrant; your hour has come!"

At every crossing and from each by-way the army was swollen.

The mass was silent, save now and then when a cheer burst from the midst, or a snatch of the "It shall go on" was sung, or cries went up of "The nation forever!"—"Long live the Breechless!"—"Down with Old Veto and Madame Veto!"

They came out for sport—to frighten the king and queen, and did not mean murdering. They demanded to march past the Assembly through the Hall, and for three hours they defiled under the eyes of their representatives.

It was three o'clock. The mob had obtained half their programme, the placing of their petition before the Assembly. The next thing was to call on the king for his sanction to the decree.

As the Assembly had received them, how could the king refuse? Surely he was not a greater potentate than the Speaker of the House, whose chair was like his and in the grander place?

In fact, the king assented to receiving their deputation of twenty.

As the common people had never entered the palace, they merely expected their representatives would be received while they marched by under the windows. They would show the king their banners with the odd devices and the gory standards.

All the palace garden gates were closed; in the yards and gardens were soldiers with four field-pieces. Seeing this apparently ample protection, the royal family might be tranquil.

Still without any evil idea, the crowd asked for the gates to be opened which allowed entrance on the Feuillants Terrace.

Three municipal officers went in and got leave from the king for passage to be given over the terrace and out by the stable doors.

Everybody wanted to go in as soon as the gates were open, and the throng spread over the lawn; it was forgotten to open the outlet by the stables, and the crush began to be severe. They streamed before the National Guards in a row along the palace wall to the Carrousel gates, by which they might have resumed the homeward route. They were locked and guarded.

Sweltering, crushed, and turned about, the mob began to be irritated. Before its growls the gates were opened and the men spread over the capacious square.

There they remembered what the main affair was—to petition the king to revoke his veto. Instead of continuing the road, they waited in the square for an hour, when they grew impatient.

They might have gone away, but that was not the aim of the agitators, who went from group to group, saying:

"Stay; what do you want to sneak away for? The king is going to give his sanction; if we were to go home without that, we should have all our work to do over again."

The level-headed thought this sensible advice, but at the same time that the sanction was a long time coming. They were getting hungry, and that was the general cry.

Bread was not so dear as it had been, but there was no work going on, and however cheap bread may be, it is not made for nothing.

Everybody had risen at five, workmen and their wives, with their children, and come to the palace with the idea that they had but to get the royal sanction to have hard times end. But the king did not seem to be at all eager to give his sanction.

It was hot, and thirst began to be felt. Hunger, thirst, and heat drive dogs mad; yet the poor people waited and kept patient. But those next to the railings set to shaking them. A municipal officer made a speech to them:

"Citizens, this is the king's residence, and to enter with arms is to violate it. The king is quite ready to receive your petition, but only from twenty deputies bearing it."

What! had not their deputation, sent in an hour ago, been attended to yet?

Suddenly loud shouts were heard on the streets. It was Santerre, Billet, and Huruge on their horses, and Theroigne riding on her cannon.

"What are you fellows hanging round this gate for?" queried Huruge. "Why do you not go right in?"

"Just so; why haven't we?" said the thousands.

"Can't you see it is fast?" cried several voices.

Theroigne jumped off her cannon, saying:

"The barker is full to the muzzle; let's blow the old gate open."

"Wait! wait!" shouted two municipal officers; "no roughness. It shall be opened to you."

Indeed, by pressing on the spring-catch they released the two gates, which drew aside, and the mass rushed through.

Along with them came the cannon, which crossed the yard with them, mounted the steps, and reached the head of the stairs in their company. Here stood the city officials in their scarfs of office.

"What do you intend doing with a piece of artillery?" they challenged. "Great guns in the royal apartments! Do you believe anything is to be gained by such violence?"

"Quite right," said the ringleaders, astonished themselves to see the gun there; and they turned it round to get it down-stairs. The hub caught on the jamb, and the muzzle gaped on the crowd.

"Why, hang them all, they have got cannon all over the palace!" commented the new-comers, not knowing their own artillery.

Police-Magistrate Mouchet, a deformed dwarf, ordered the men to chop the wheel clear, and they managed to hack the door-jamb away so as to free the piece, which was taken down to the yard. This led to the report that the mob were smashing all the doors in.

Some two hundred noblemen ran to the palace, not with the hope of defending it, but to die with the king, whose life they deemed menaced. Prominent among these was a man in black, who had previously offered his breast to the assassin's bullet, and who always leaped like a last Life-Guard between danger and the king, from whom he had tried to conjure it. This was Gilbert.

After being excited by the frightful tumult, the king and queen became used to it.

It was half past three, and it was hoped that the day would close with no more harm done.

Suddenly, the sound of the ax blows was heard above the noise of clamor, like the howling of a coming tempest. A man darted into the king's sleeping-room and called out:

"Sire, let me stand by you, and I will answer for all."

It was Dr. Gilbert, seen at almost periodical intervals, and in all the "striking situations" of the tragedy in play.

"Oh, doctor, is this you? What is it?" King and queen spoke together.

"The palace is surrounded, and the people are making this uproar in wanting to see you."

"We shall not leave you, sire," said the queen and Princess Elizabeth.

"Will the king kindly allow me for an hour such power as a captain has over his ship?" asked Gilbert.

"I grant it," replied the monarch. "Madame, hearken to Doctor Gilbert's advice, and obey his orders, if needs must." He turned to the doctor: "Will you answer to me for the queen and the dauphin?"

"I do, or I shall die with them; it is all a pilot can say in the tempest!"

The queen wished to make a last effort, but Gilbert barred the way with his arms.

"Madame," he said, "it is you and not the king who run the real danger. Rightly or wrongly, they accuse you of the king's resistance, so that your presence will expose him without defending him. Be the lightning-conductor—divert the bolt, if you can!"

"Then let it fall on me, but save my children!"

"I have answered for you and them to the king. Follow me."

He said the same to Princess Lamballe, who had returned lately from London, and the other ladies, and guided them to the Council Hall, where he placed them in a window recess, with the heavy table before them.

The queen stood behind her children—Innocence protecting Unpopularity, although she wished it to be the other way.

"All is well thus," said Gilbert, in the tone of a general commanding a decisive operation; "do not stir."

There came a pounding at the door, which he threw open with both folds, and as he knew there were many women in the crowd, he cried:

"Walk in, citizenesses; the queen and her children await you."

The crowd burst in as through a broken dam.

"Where is the Austrian? where is the Lady Veto?" demanded five hundred voices.

It was the critical moment.

"Be calm," said Gilbert to the queen, knowing that all was in Heaven's hand, and man was as nothing. "I need not recommend you to be kind."

Preceding the others was a woman with her hair down, who brandished a saber; she was flushed with rage—perhaps from hunger.

"Where is the Austrian cat? She shall die by no hand but mine!" she screamed.

"This is she," said Gilbert, taking her by the hand and leading her up to the queen.

"Have I ever done you a personal wrong?" demanded the latter, in her sweetest voice.

"I can not say you have," faltered the woman of the people, amazed at the majesty and gentleness of Marie Antoinette.

"Then why should you wish to kill me?"

"Folks told me that you were the ruin of the nation," faltered the abashed young woman, lowering the point of her saber to the floor.

"Then you were told wrong. I married your King of France, and am mother of the prince whom you see here. I am a French woman, one who will nevermore see the land where she was born; in France alone I must dwell, happy or unhappy. Alas! I was happy when you loved me." And she sighed.

The girl dropped the sword, and wept.

"Beg your pardon, madame, but I did not know what you were like. I see you are a good sort, after all."

"Keep on like that," prompted Gilbert, "and not only will you be saved, but all these people will be at your feet in an hour."

Intrusting her to some National Guardsmen and the War Minister, who came in with the mob, he ran to the king.

Louis had gone through a similar experience. On hastening toward the crowd, as he opened the Bull's-eye Room, the door panels were dashed in, and pikes, bayonets, and axes showed their points and edges.

"Open the doors!" cried the king.

Servants heaped up chairs before him, and four grenadiers stood in front, but he made them put up their swords, as the flash of steel might seem a provocation.

A ragged fellow, with a knife-blade set in a pole, darted at the king, yelling:

"Take that for your veto!"

One grenadier, who had not yet sheathed his sword, struck down the stick with the blade. But it was the king who, entirely recovering self-command, put the soldier aside with his hand, and said:

"Let me stand forward, sir. What have I to fear amid my people?"

Taking a forward step, Louis XVI., with a majesty not expected in him, and a courage strange heretofore in him, offered his breast to the weapons of all sorts directed against him.

"Hold your noise!" thundered a stentorian voice in the midst of the awful din. "I want a word in here."

A cannon might have vainly sought to be heard in this clamor, but at this voice all the vociferation ceased. This was the butcher Legendre. He went up almost to touching the king, while they formed a ring round the two.

Just then, on the outer edge of the circle, a man made his appearance, and behind the dread double of Danton, the king recognized Gilbert, pale and serene of face. The questioning glance implying: "What have you done with the queen?" was answered by the doctor's smile to the effect that she was in safety. He thanked him with a nod.

"Sirrah," began Legendre.

This expression, which seemed to indicate that the sovereign was already deposed, made the latter turn as if a snake had stung him.

"Yes, sir, I am talking to you, Veto," went on Legendre. "Just listen to us, for it is our turn to have you hear us. You are a double-dealer, who have always cheated us, and would try it again, so look out for yourself. The measure is full, and the people are tired of being your plaything and victim."

"Well, I am listening to you, sir," rejoined the king.

"And a good thing, too. Do you know what we have come here for? To ask the sanction of the decrees and the recall of the ministers. Here is our petition—see!"

Taking a paper from his pocket, he unfolded it, and read the same menacing lines which had been heard in the House. With his eyes fixed on the speaker, the king listened, and said, when it was ended, without the least apparent emotion:

"Sir, I shall do what the laws and the Constitution order me to do!"

"Gammon!" broke in a voice; "the Constitution is your high horse, which lets you block the road of the whole country, to keep France in-doors, for fear of being trampled on, and wait till the Austrians come up to cut her throat."

The king turned toward this fresh voice, comprehending that it was a worse danger. Gilbert also made a movement and laid his hand on the speaker's shoulder.

"I have seen you somewhere before, friend," remarked the king. "Who are you?"

He looked with more curiosity than fear, though this man wore a front of terrible resolution.

"Ay, you have seen me before, sire. Three times: once, when you were brought back from Versailles; next at Varennes; and the last time, here. Sire, bear my name in mind, for it is of ill omen. It is Billet."

At this the shouting was renewed, and a man with a lance tried to stab the king; but Billet seized the weapon, tore it from the wielder's grip, and snapped it across his knee.

"No foul play," he said; "only one kind of steel has the right to touch this man: the ax of the executioner! I hear that a King of England had his head cut off by the people whom he betrayed—you ought to know his name, Louis. Don't you forget it."

"'Sh, Billet!" muttered Gilbert.

"Oh, you may say what you like," returned Billet, shaking his head; "this man is going to be tried and doomed as a traitor."

"Yes, a traitor!" yelled a hundred voices; "traitor, traitor!"

Gilbert threw himself in between.

"Fear nothing, sire, and try by some material token to give satisfaction to these mad men."

Taking the physician's hand, the king laid it on his heart.

"You see that I fear nothing," he said; "I received the sacraments this morning. Let them do what they like with me. As for the material sign which you suggest I should display—are you satisfied?"

Taking the red cap from a by-stander, he set it on his own head. The multitude burst into applause.

"Hurrah for the king!" shouted all the voices.

A fellow broke through the crowd and held up a bottle.

"If fat old Veto loves the people as much as he says, prove it by drinking our health."

"Do not drink," whispered a voice. "It may be poisoned."

"Drink, sire, I answer for the honesty," said Gilbert.

The king took the bottle, and saying, "To the health of the people," he drank. Fresh cheers for the king resounded.

"Sire, you have nothing to fear," said Gilbert; "allow me to return to the queen."

"Go," said the other, gripping his hand.

More tranquil, the doctor hastened to the Council Hall, where he breathed still easier after one glance. The queen stood in the same spot; the little prince, like his father, was wearing the red cap.

In the next room was a great hubbub; it was the reception of Santerre, who rolled into the hall.

"Where is this Austrian wench?" demanded he.

Gilbert cut slanting across the hall to intercept him.

"Halloo, Doctor Gilbert!" said he, quite joyfully.

"Who has not forgotten that you were one of those who opened the Bastile doors to me," replied the doctor. "Let me present you to the queen."

"Present me to the queen?" growled the brewer.

"You will not refuse, will you?"

"Faith, I'll not. I was going to introduce myself; but as you are in the way—"

"Monsieur Santerre needs no introduction," interposed the queen. "I know how at the famine time he fed at his sole expense half the St. Antoine suburb."

Santerre stopped, astonished; then, his glance happening to fall, embarrassed, on the dauphin, whose perspiration was running down his cheeks, he roared:

"Here, take that sweater off the boy—don't you see he is smothering?"

The queen thanked him with a look. He leaned on the table, and bending toward her, he said in an under-tone:

"You have a lot of clumsy friends, madame. I could tell you of some who would serve you better."

An hour afterward all the mob had flowed away, and the king, accompanied by his sister, entered the room where the queen and his children awaited him.

She ran to him and threw herself at his feet, while the children seized his hands, and all acted as though they had been saved from a shipwreck. It was only then that the king noticed that he was wearing the red cap.

"Faugh!" he said; "I had forgotten!"

Snatching it off with both hands, he flung it far from him with disgust.

The evacuation of the palace was as dull and dumb as the taking had been gleeful and noisy. Astonished at the little result, the mob said:

"We have not made anything; we shall have to come again."

In fact, it was too much for a threat, and not enough for an attempt on the king's life.

Louis had been judged on his reputation, and recalling his flight to Varennes, disguised as a serving-man, they had thought that he would hide under a table at the first noise, and might be done to death in the scuffle, like Polonius behind the arras.

Things had happened otherwise; never had the monarch been calmer, never so grand. In the height of the threats and the insults he had not ceased to say: "Behold your king!"

The Royalists were delighted, for, to tell the truth, they had carried the day.

CHAPTER VI. "THE COUNTRY IS IN DANGER!"

The king wrote to the Assembly to complain of the violation of his residence, and he issued a proclamation to "his people." So it appeared there were two peoples—the king's, and those he complained of.

On the twenty-fourth, the king and queen were cheered by the National Guards, whom they were reviewing, and on this same day, the Paris Directory suspended Mayor Petion, who had told the king to his face that the city was not riotous.

Whence sprung such audacity?

Three days after, the murder was out.

Lafayette came to beard the Assembly in its House, taunted by a member, who had said, when he wrote to encourage the king in his opposition and to daunt the representatives:

"He is very saucy in the midst of his army; let us see if he would talk as big if he stood among us."

He escaped censure by a nominal majority—a victory worse than a defeat.

Lafayette had again sacrificed his popularity for the Royalists.

He cherished a last hope. With the enthusiasm to be kindled among the National Guards by the king and their old commander, he proposed to march on the Assembly and put down the Opposition, while in the confusion the king should gain the camp at Maubeuge.

It was a bold scheme, but was almost sure in the state of minds.

Unfortunately, Danton ran to Petion at three in the morning with the news, and the review was countermanded.

Who had betrayed the king and the general? The queen, who had said she would rather be lost than owe safety to Lafayette.

She was helping fate, for she was doomed to be slain by Danton.

But supposing she had less spite, and the Girondists might have been crushed. They were determined not to be caught napping another time.

It was necessary to restore the revolutionary current to its old course, for it had been checked and was running up-stream.

The soul of the party, Mme. Roland, hoped to do this by rousing the Assembly. She chose the orator Vergniaud to make the appeal, and in a splendid speech, he shouted from the rostrum what was already circulating in an under-tone:

"The country is in danger!"

The effect was like a waterspout; the whole House, even to the Royalists, spectators, officials, all were enveloped and carried away by this mighty cyclone; all roared with enthusiasm.

That same evening Barbaroux wrote to his friend Rebecqui, at Marseilles:

"Send me five hundred men eager to die."

On the eleventh of July, the Assembly declared the country to be in danger, but the king withheld his authorization until the twenty-first, late at night. Indeed, this call to arms was an admission that the ruler was impotent, for the nation would not be asked to help herself unless the king could or would do nothing.

Great terror made the palace quiver in the interval, as a plot was expected to break out on the fourteenth, the anniversary of the taking of the Bastile—a holiday.

Robespierre had sent an address out from the Jacobin Club which suggested regicide.

So persuaded was the Court party, that the king was induced to wear a shirt of mail to protect him against the assassin's knife, and Mme. Campan had another for the queen, who refused to don it.

"I should be only too happy if they would slay me," she observed, in a low voice. "Oh, God, they would do me a greater kindness than Thou didst in giving me life! they would relieve me of a burden!"

Mme. Campan went out, choking. The king, who was in the corridor, took her by the hand and led her into the lobby between his rooms and his son's, and stopping, groped for a secret spring; it opened a press, perfectly hidden in the wall, with the edges guarded by the moldings. A large portfolio of papers was in the closet, with gold coin on the shelves.

The case of papers was so heavy that the lady could not lift it, and the king carried it to her rooms, saying that the queen would tell her how to dispose of it. She thrust it between the bed and the mattress, and went to the queen, who said:

"Campan, those are documents fatal to the king if he were placed on trial, which the Lord forbid. Particularly—which is why, no doubt, he confides it all to you—there is a report of a council, in which the king gave his opinion against war; he made all the ministers sign it, and reckons on this document being as beneficial in event of a trial as the others may be hurtful."

The July festival arrived. The idea was to celebrate the triumph of Petion over the king—that of murdering the latter not being probably entertained.

Suspended in his functions by the Assembly, Petion was restored to them on the eve of the rejoicings.

At eleven in the morning, the king came down the grand staircase with the queen and the royal children. Three or four thousand troops, of unknown tendencies, escorted them. In vain did the queen seek on their faces some marks of sympathy; the kindest averted their faces.

There was no mistaking the feeling of the crowd, for cheers for Petion rose on all sides. As if, too, to give the ovation a more durable stamp than momentary enthusiasm, the king and the queen could read on all hats a lettered ribbon: "Petion forever!"

The queen was pale and trembling. Convinced that a plot was aimed at her husband's life, she started at every instant, fancying she saw a hand thrust out to bring down a dagger or level a pistol.

On the parade-ground, the monarch alighted, took a place on the left of the Speaker of the House, and with him walked up to the Altar of the Country. The queen had to separate from her lord here to go into the grand stand with her children; she stopped, refusing to go any further until she saw how he got on, and kept her eyes on him.

At the foot of the altar, one of those rushes came which is common to great gatherings. The king disappeared as though submerged.

The queen shrieked, and made as if to rush to him; but he rose into view anew, climbing the steps of the altar.

Among the ordinary symbols figuring in these feasts, such as justice, power, liberty, etc., one glittered mysteriously and dreadfully under black crape, carried by a man clad in black and crowned with cypress. This weird emblem particularly caught the queen's eyes. She was riveted to the spot, and, while encouraged a little by the king's fate, she could not take her gaze from this somber apparition. Making an effort to speak, she gasped, without addressing any one specially:

"Who is that man dressed in mourning?"

"The death's-man," replied a voice which made her shudder.

"And what has he under the veil?" continued she.

"The ax which chopped off the head of King Charles I."

The queen turned round, losing color, for she thought she recognized the voice. She was not mistaken; the speaker was the magician who had shown her the awful future in a glass at Taverney, and warned her at Sèvres and on her return from Varennes—Cagliostro, in fact.

She screamed, and fell fainting into Princess Elizabeth's arms.

One week subsequently, on the twenty-second, at six in the morning, all

Paris was aroused by the first of a series of minute guns. The terrible booming went on all through the day.

At day-break the six legions of the National Guards were collected at the City Hall. Two processions were formed throughout the town and suburbs to spread the proclamation that the country was in danger.

Danton had the idea of this dreadful show, and he had intrusted the details to Sergent, the engraver, an immense stage-manager.

Each party left the Hall at six o'clock.

First marched a cavalry squadron, with the mounted band playing a funeral march, specially composed. Next, six field-pieces, abreast where the road-way was wide enough, or in pairs. Then four heralds on horseback, bearing ensigns labeled "Liberty"—"Equality"—"Constitution"—"Our Country." Then came twelve city officials, with swords by the sides and their scarfs on. Then, all alone, isolated like France herself, a National Guardsman, in the saddle of a black horse, holding a large tri-color flag, on which was lettered:

"CITIZENS, THE COUNTRY IS IN DANGER!"

In the same order as the preceding, rolled six guns with weighty jolting and heavy rumbling, National Guards and cavalry at the rear.

On every bridge, crossing, and square, the party halted, and silence was commanded by the ruffling of the drums. The banners were waved, and when no sound was heard and the crowd held their peace, the grave voice of the municipal crier arose, reading the proclamation, and adding:

"The country is in danger!"

This last line was dreadful, and rang in all hearts. It was the shriek of the nation, of the motherland, of France. It was the parent calling on her offspring to help her.

And ever and anon the guns kept thundering.

On all the large open places platforms were run up for the voluntary enlistments. With the intoxication of patriotism, the men rushed to put their names down. Some were too old, but lied to be inscribed; some too young, but stood on tiptoe and swore they were full sixteen.

Those who were accepted leaped to the ground, waving their enrollment papers, and cheering or singing the "Let it go on," and kissing the cannon's mouth.

It was the betrothal of the French to war—this war of twenty odd years, which will result in the freedom of Europe, although it may not altogether be in our time.

The excitement was so great that the Assembly was appalled by its own work; it sent men through the town to cry out: "Brothers, for the sake of the country, no rioting! The court wishes disorder as an excuse for taking the king out of the city, so give it no pretext. The king should stay among us."

These dread sowers of words added in a deep voice:

"He must be punished."

They mentioned nobody by name, but all knew who was meant.

Every cannon-report had an echo in the heart of the palace. Those were the king's rooms where the queen and the rest of the family were gathered. They kept together all day, from feeling that their fate was decided this time, so grand and solemn. They did not separate until midnight, when the last cannon was fired.

On the following night Mme. Campan was aroused; she had slept in the queen's bedroom since a fellow had been caught there with a knife, who might have been a murderer.

"Is your majesty ill?" she asked, hearing a moan.

"I am always in pain, Campan, but I trust to have it over soon now. Yes," and she held out her pale hand in the moonbeam, making it seem all the whiter, "in a month this same moonlight will see us free and disengaged from our chains."

66

"Oh, you have accepted Lafayette's offers," said the lady, "and you will flee?"

"Lafayette's help? Thank God, no," said the queen, with repugnance there was no mistaking; "no, but in a month, my nephew, Francis, will be in Paris."

"Is your majesty quite sure?" asked the royal governess, alarmed.

"Yes, all is settled," returned the sovereign; "alliance is made between Austria and Prussia, two powers who will march upon Paris in combination. We have the route of the French princes and their allied armies, and we can surely say that on such and such a day they will be here or there."

"But do you not fear—"

"Murder?" The queen finished the phrase. "I know that might befall; but they may hold us as hostages for their necks when vengeance impends. However, nothing venture, nothing win."

"And when do the allied sovereigns expect to be in Paris?" inquired Mme. Campan.

"Between the fifteenth and twentieth of August," was the reply.

"God grant it!" said the lady.

But the prayer was not granted; or, if heard, Heaven sent France the succor she had not dreamed of—the Marseillaise Hymn of Liberty.

CHAPTER VII. THE MEN FROM MARSEILLES.

We have said that Barbaroux had written to a friend in the south to send him five hundred men willing to die.

Who was the man who could write such lines? and what influence had he over his friends?

Charles Barbaroux was a very handsome young man of barely twenty-five, who was reproached for his beauty, and considered by Mme. Roland as frivolous and too generally amorous. On the contrary, he loved his country alone, or must have loved her best, for he died for her.

Son of a hardy sea-faring man, he was a poet and orator when quite young—at the breaking out of trouble in his native town during the election of Mirabeau. He was then appointed secretary to the Marseilles town board. Riots at Arles drew him into them; but the seething caldron of Paris claimed him; the immense furnace which needed perfume, the huge crucible hissing for purest metal.

He was Roland's correspondent at the south, and Mme. Roland had pictured from his regular, precise, and wise letters, a man of forty, with his head bald from much thinking, and his forehead wrinkled with vigils. The reality of her dream was a young man, gay, merry, light, fond of her sex, the type of the rich and brilliant generation flourishing in '92, to be cut down in '93.

It was in this head, esteemed too frivolous by Mme. Roland, that the first thought of the tenth of August was conceived, perhaps.

The storm was in the air, but the clouds were tossing about in all directions for Barbaroux to give them a direction and pile them up over the Tuileries.

When nobody had a settled plan, he wrote for five hundred determined men.

The true ruler of France was the man who could write for such men and be sure of their coming.

Rebecqui chose them himself out of the revolutionists who had fought in the last two years' popular affrays, in Avignon and the other fiery towns; they were used to blood; they did not know what fatigue was by name.

On the appointed day they set out on the two hundred league tramp, as if it were a day's strolling. Why not? They were hardy seamen, rugged peasants, sunburned by the African simoom or the mountain gale, with hands callous from the spade or tough with tar.

Wherever they passed along they were hailed as brigands.

In a halt they received the words and music of Rouget de l'Isle's "Hymn to Liberty," sent as a viaticum by Barbaroux to shorten the road. The lips of the Marseilles men made it change in character, while the words were altered by their new emphasis. The song of brotherhood became one of death and extermination—forever "the Marseillaise."

Barbaroux had planned to head with the Marseilles men some forty thousand volunteers Santerre was to have ready to meet them, overwhelm the City Hall and the House, and then storm the palace. But Santerre went to greet them with only two hundred men, not liking to let the strangers have the glory of such a rush.

With ardent eyes, swart visages, and shrill voices, the little band strode through all Paris to the Champs Elysées, singing the thrilling song. They camped there, awaiting the banquet on the morrow.

It took place, but some grenadiers were arrayed close to the spot, a Royalist guard set as a rampart between them and the palace.

They divined they were enemies, and commencing by insults, they went on to exchanging fisticuffs. At the first blood the Marseillaise shouted "To arms!" raided the stacks of muskets, and sent the grenadiers flying with their own bayonets. Luckily, they had the Tuileries at their backs and got over the draw-bridge, finding shelter in the royal apartments. There is a legend that the queen bound up the wounds of one soldier.

The Federals numbered five thousand—Marseilles men, Bretons, and Dauphinois. They were a power, not from their number, but their faith. The spirit of the revolution was in them.

They had fire-arms but no ammunition; they called for cartridges, but none were supplied. Two of them went to the mayor and demanded powder, or they would kill themselves in the office.

Two municipal officers were on duty—Sergent, Danton's man, and Panis, Robespierre's.

Sergent had artistic imagination and a French heart; he felt that the young men spoke with the voice of the country.

"Look out, Panis," he said; "if these youths kill themselves, the blood will fall on our heads."

"But if we deliver the powder without authorization, we risk our necks."

"Never mind. I believe the time has come to risk our necks. In that case, everybody for himself," replied Sergent. "Here goes for mine; you can do as you like."

He signed the delivery note, and Panis put his name to it.

Things were easier now; when the Marseilles men had powder and shot they would not let themselves be butchered without hitting back.

As soon as they were armed, the Assembly received their petition, and allowed them to attend the session. The Assembly was in great fear, so much so as to debate whether it ought not to transfer the meetings to the country. For everybody stood in doubt, feeling the ground to quake underfoot and fearing to be swallowed.

This wavering chafed the southerners. No little disheartened, Barbaroux talked of founding a republic in the south.

He turned to Robespierre, to see if he would help to set the ball rolling.

But the Incorruptible's conditions gave him suspicions, and he left him, saying:

"We will no more have a dictator than a king."

CHAPTER VIII. THE FRIEND IN NEED.

The very thing encouraging the Tuileries party was what awed the rebels.

The palace had become a formidable fortress, with a dreadful garrison.

During the night of the fourth of August, the Swiss battalions had been drawn from out of town into the palace. A few companies were left at Gaillon, where the king might take refuge.

Three reliable leaders were beside the queen: Maillardet with his Switzers, Hervilly with the St. Louis Knights and the Constitutional Guard, and Mandat, who, as National Guard commander, promised twenty thousand devoted and resolute fighting men.

On the evening of the eighth a man penetrated the fort; everybody knew him, so that he had no difficulty in passing to the queen's rooms, where they announced "Doctor Gilbert."

"Ah, welcome, welcome, doctor!" said the royal lady, in a feverish voice, "I am happy to see you."

He looked sharply at her, for on the whole of her face was such gladness and satisfaction that it made him shudder. He would sooner have seen her pale and disheartened.

"I fear I have arrived too late," he said.

"It is just the other way, doctor," she replied, with a smile, an expression her lips had almost forgotten how to make; "you come at the right time, and you are welcome. You are going to see what I have long yearned to show you—a king really royal."

"I am afraid, madame, that you are deceiving yourself," he returned, "and that you will exhibit rather the commandant of a fort."

"Perhaps, Doctor Gilbert, we can never come to a closer understanding on the symbolical character of royalty than on other matters. For me a king is not solely a man who may say, 'I do not wish,' but one who can say, 'Thus I will.'"

She alluded to the famous veto which led to this crisis.

"Yes, madame," said Gilbert, "and for your majesty, a king is a ruler who takes revenge."

"Who defends himself," she retorted; "for you know we are openly threatened, and are to be attacked by an armed force. We are assured that five hundred desperadoes from Marseilles, headed by one Barbaroux, took an oath on the ruins of the Bastile, not to go home until they had camped on the ruins of the Tuileries."

"Indeed, I have heard something of the kind," remarked Gilbert.

"Which only makes you laugh?"

"It alarms me for the king and yourself, madame."

"So that you come to propose that we should resign, and place ourselves at the mercy of Messieurs Barbaroux and his Marseilles bullies?"

"I only wish the king could abdicate and guarantee, by the sacrifice of his crown, his life and yours, and the safety of your children."

"Is this the advice you give us, doctor?"

"It is; and I humbly beseech you to follow it."

"Monsieur Gilbert, let me say that you are not consistent in your opinions."

"My opinions are always the same, madame. Devoted to king and country, I wished him to be in accord with the Constitution; from this desire springs the different pieces of counsel which I have submitted."

"What is the one you fit to this juncture?"

"One that you have never had such a good chance to follow. I say, get away."

"Flee?"

"Ah, you well know that it is possible, and never could be carried out with greater facility. You have nearly three thousand men in the palace."

"Nearer five thousand," said the queen, with a smile of satisfaction, "with double to rise at the first signal we give."

"You have no need to give a signal, which may be intercepted; the five thousand will suffice."

"What do you think we ought to do with them?"

"Set yourself in their midst, with the king and your august children; dash out when least expected; at a couple of leagues out, take to horse and ride into Normandy, to Gaillon, where you are looked for."

"You mean, place ourselves under the thumb of General Lafayette?"

"At least, he has proved that he is devoted to you."

"No, sir, no! With my five thousand in hand, and as many more ready to come at the call, I like another course better—to crush this revolt once for all."

"Oh, madame, how right he was who said you were doomed."

"Who was that, sir?"

"A man whose name I dare not repeat to you; but he has spoken three times to you."

"Silence!" said the queen, turning pale; "we will try to give the lie to this prophet of evil."

"Madame, I am very much afraid that you are blinded."

"You think that they will venture to attack us?"

"The public spirit turns to this quarter."

"And they reckon on walking in here as easily as they did in June?"

"This is not a stronghold."

"Nay; but if you will come with me, I will show you that we can hold out some time."

With joy and pride she showed him all the defensive measures of the military engineers and the number of the garrison whom she believed faithful.

"That is a comfort, madame," he said, "but it is not security."

"You frown on everything, let me tell you, doctor."

"Your majesty has taken me round where you like; will you let me take you to your own rooms, now?"

"Willingly, doctor, for I am tired. Give me your arm."

Gilbert bowed to have this high favor, most rarely granted by the sovereign, even to her intimate friends, especially since her misfortune.

When they were in her sitting-room he dropped on one knee to her as she took a seat in an arm-chair.

"Madame," said he, "let me adjure you, in the name of your august husband, your dear ones, your own safety, to make use of the forces about you, to flee and not to fight."

"Sir," was the reply, "since the fourteenth of July, I have been aspiring for the king to have his revenge; I believe the time has come. We will save royalty, or bury ourselves under the ruins of the Tuileries."

"Can nothing turn you from this fatal resolve?"

"Nothing."

She held out her hand to him, half to help him to rise, half to send him away. He kissed her hand respectfully, and rising, said:

"Will your majesty permit me to write a few lines which I regard as so urgent that I do not wish to delay one instant?"

"Do so, sir," she said, pointing to a writing-table, where he sat down and wrote these lines:

> "My Lord,—Come! the queen is in danger of death, if a friend does not persuade her to flee, and I believe you are the only one who can have that influence over her."

"May I ask whom you are writing to, without being too curious?" demanded the lady.

"To the Count of Charny, madame," was Gilbert's reply.

"And why do you apply to him?"

"For him to obtain from your majesty what I fail to do."

"Count Charny is too happy to think of his unfortunate friends; he will not come," said the queen.

The door opened, and an usher appeared.

"The Right Honorable, the Count of Charny," he announced, "desiring to learn if he may present his respects to your majesty."

The queen had been pale, and now became corpse-like, as she stammered some unintelligible words.

"Let him enter," said Gilbert; "Heaven hath sent him."

Charny appeared at the door in naval officer's uniform.

"Oh, come in, sir; I was writing for you," said the physician, handing him the note.

"Hearing of the danger her majesty was incurring, I came," said the nobleman, bowing.

"Madame, for Heaven's sake, hear and heed what Count Charny says," said Gilbert; "his voice will be that of France."

Respectfully saluting the lord and the royal lady, Gilbert went out, still cherishing a last hope.

CHAPTER IX. CHARNY ON GUARD.

On the night of the ninth of August, the royal family supped as usual; nothing could disturb the king in his meals. But while Princess Elizabeth and Lady Lamballe wept and prayed, the queen prayed without weeping. The king withdrew to go to confession.

At this time the doors opened, and Count Charny walked in, pale, but perfectly calm.

"May I have speech with the king?" he asked, as he bowed.

"At present I am the king," answered Marie Antoinette.

Charny knew this as well as anybody, but he persisted.

"You may go up to the king's rooms, count, but I protest that you will very much disturb him."

"I understand; he is with Mayor Petion."

"The king is with his ghostly counselor," replied the lady, with an indescribable expression.

"Then I must make my report to your majesty as major-general of the castle," said the count.

"Yes, if you will kindly do so."

"I have the honor to set forth the effective strength of our forces. The heavy horse-guards, under Rulhieres and Verdiere, to the number of six hundred, are in battle array on the Louvre grand square; the Paris City foot-guards are barracked in the stables; a hundred and fifty are drawn from them to guard at Toulouse House, at need, the Treasury and the discount and extra cash offices; the Paris Mounted Patrol, only thirty men, are posted in the princes' yard, at the foot of the king's back stairs; two hundred officers and men of the old Life Guards, a hundred young Royalists, as many noblemen, making some four hundred combatants, are in the Bull's-eye Hall and adjoining rooms; two or three hundred National Guards are scattered in the gardens and court-yards; and lastly, fifteen hundred Swiss, the backbone of resistance, are taking position under the grand vestibule and the staircases which they are charged to defend."

"Do not all these measures set you at ease, my lord?" inquired the queen.

"Nothing can set me at ease when your majesty's safety is at stake," returned the count.

"Then your advice is still for flight?"

"My advice, madame, is that you ought, with the king and the royal children, be in the midst of us."

The queen shook her head.

"Your majesty dislikes Lafayette? Be it so. But you have confidence in the Duke of Liancourt, who is in Rouen, in the house of an English gentleman of the name of Canning. The commander of the troops in that province has made them swear allegiance to the king; the Salis-Chamade Swiss regiment is echeloned across the road, and it may be relied on. All is still quiet. Let us get out over the swing-bridge, and reach the Etoille bars, where three hundred of the horse-guards await us. At Versailles, we can readily get together fifteen hundred noblemen. With four thousand, I answer for taking you wherever you like to go."

"I thank you, Lord Charny. I appreciate the devotion which made you leave those dear to you, to offer your services to a foreigner."

"The queen is unjust toward me," replied Charny. "My sovereign's existence is always the most precious of all in my eyes, as duty is always the dearest of virtues."

"Duty—yes, my lord," murmured the queen; "but I believe I understand my own when everybody is bent on doing theirs. It is to maintain royalty grand and noble, and to have it fall worthily, like the ancient gladiators, who studied how to die with grace."

"Is this your majesty's last word?"

"It is—above all, my last desire."

Charny bowed, and as he met Mme. Campan by the door, he said to her:

"Suggest to the princesses that they should put all their valuables in their pockets, as they may have to quit the palace without further warning."

While the governess went to speak to the ladies, he returned to the queen, and said:

"Madame, it is impossible that you should not have some hope beyond the reliance on material forces. Confide in me, for you will please bear in mind that at such a strait, I will have to give an account to the Maker and to man for what will have happened."

"Well, my lord," said the queen, "an agent is to pay Petion two hundred thousand francs, and Danton fifty thousand, for which sums the latter is to stay at home and the other is to come to the palace."

"Are you sure of the go-betweens?"

"You said that Petion had come, which is something toward it."

"Hardly enough; as I understood that he had to be sent for three times."

"The token is, in speaking to the king, he is to touch his right eyebrow with his forefinger—"

"But if not arranged?"

"He will be our prisoner, and I have given the most positive orders that he is not to be let quit the palace."

The ringing of a bell was heard.

"What is that?" inquired the queen.

"The general alarm," rejoined Charny.

The princesses rose in alarm.

"What is the matter?" exclaimed the queen. "The tocsin is always the trumpet of rebellion."

"Madame," said Charny, more affected by the sinister sound than the queen, "I had better go and learn whether the alarm means anything grave."

"But we shall see you again?" asked she, quickly.

"I came to take your majesty's orders, and I shall not leave you until you are out of danger."

Bowing, he went out. The queen stood pensive for a space, murmuring: "I suppose we had better see if the king has got through confessing."

While she was going out, Princess Elizabeth took some garments off a sofa in order to lie down with more comfort; from her fichu she removed a cornelian brooch, which she showed to Mme. Campan; the engraved stone had a bunch of lilies and the motto: "Forget offenses, forgive injuries."

"I fear that this will have little influence over our enemies," she remarked; "but it ought not be the less dear to us."

As she was finishing the words, a gunshot was heard in the yard.

The ladies screamed.

"There goes the first shot," said Lady Elizabeth. "Alas! it will not be the last."

Mayor Petion had come into the palace under the following circumstances. He arrived about half past ten. He was not made to wait, as had happened before, but was told that the king was ready to see him; but to arrive, he had to walk through a double row of Swiss guards, National Guards, and those volunteer royalists called Knights of the Dagger. Still, as they knew he had been sent for, they merely cast the epithets of "traitor" and "Judas" in his face as he went up the stairs.

Petion smiled as he went in at the door of the room, for here the king had given him the lie on the twentieth of June; he was going to have ample revenge.

The king was impatiently awaiting.

80

"Ah! so you have come, Mayor Petion?" he said. "What is the good word from Paris?"

Petion furnished the account of the state of matters—or, at least, an account.

"Have you nothing more to tell me?" demanded the ruler.

"No," replied Petion, wondering why the other stared at him. Louis watched for the signal that the mayor had accepted the bribe.

It was clear that the king had been cheated; some swindler had pocketed the money. The queen came in as the question was put to Petion.

"How does our friend stand?" she whispered.

"He has not made any sign," rejoined the king.

"Then he is our prisoner," said she.

"Can I retire?" inquired the mayor.

"For God's sake, do not let him go!" interposed the queen.

"Not yet, sir; I have something yet to say to you," responded the king, raising his voice. "Pray step into this closet."

This implied to those in the inner room that Petion was intrusted to them, and was not to be allowed to go.

Those in the room understood perfectly, and surrounded Petion, who felt that he was a prisoner. He was the thirtieth in a room where there was not elbow-room for four.

"Why, gentlemen, we are smothering here," he said; "I propose a change of air."

It was a sentiment all agreed with, and they followed him out of the first door he opened, and down into the walled-in garden, where he was as much confined as in the closet. To kill time, he picked up a pebble or two and tossed them over the walls.

While he was playing thus, and chatting with Roederer, attorney of the province, the message came twice that the king wanted to see him.

"No," replied Petion; "it is too hot quarters up there. I remember the closet, and I have no eagerness to be in it again. Besides, I have an appointment with somebody on the Feuillants' Quay."

He went on playing at clearing the wall with stones.

"With whom have you an appointment?" asked Roederer.

At this instant the Assembly door on the Feuillants' Quay opened.

"I fancy this is just what I was waiting for," remarked the mayor.

"Order to let Mayor Petion pass forth," said a voice; "the Assembly demands his presence at the bar of the House, to give an account of the state of the city."

"Just the thing," muttered Petion. "Here I am," he replied, in a loud voice; "I am ready to respond to the quips of my enemies."

The National Guards, imagining that Petion was to be berated, let him out.

It was nearly three in the morning; the day was breaking. A singular thing, the aurora was the hue of blood.

CHAPTER X. BILLET AND PITOU.

On being called by the king, Petion had foreseen that he might more easily get into the palace than out, so he went up to a hard-faced man marred by a scar on the brow.

"Farmer Billet," said he, "what was your report about the House?"

"That it would hold an all-night sitting."

"Very good; and what did you say you saw on the New Bridge?"

"Cannon and Guards, placed by order of Colonel Mandat."

"And you also stated that a considerable force was collected under St. John's Arcade, near the opening of St. Antoine Street?"

"Yes; again, by order of Colonel Mandat."

"Well, will you listen to me? Here you have an order to Manuel and Danton to send back to barracks the troops at St. John's Arcade, and to remove the guns from the bridge; at any cost, you will understand, these orders must be obeyed."

"I will hand it to Danton myself."

"Good. You are living in St. Honore Street?"

"Yes, mayor."

"When you have given Danton the order, get home and snatch a bit of rest. About two o'clock, go out to the Feuillants' Quay, where you will stand by the wall. If you see or hear stones falling over from the other side of the wall, it will mean that I am a prisoner in the Tuileries, and detained by violence."

"I understand."

"Present yourself at the bar of the House, and ask my colleagues to claim me. You understand, Farmer Billet, I am placing my life in your hands."

"I will answer for it," replied the bluff farmer; "take it easy."

Petion had therefore gone into the lion's den, relying on Billet's patriotism.

The latter had spoken the more firmly, as Pitou had come to town. He dispatched the young peasant to Danton, with the word for him not to return without him. Lazy as the orator was, Pitou had a prevailing way, and he brought Danton with him.

Danton had seen the cannon on the bridge, and the National Guards at the end of the popular quarter, and he understood the urgency of not leaving such forces on the rear of the people's army. With Petion's order in hand, he and Manuel sent the Guards away and removed the guns.

This cleared the road for the Revolution.

In the meantime, Billet and Pitou had gone to their old lodging in St. Honore Street, to which Pitou bobbed his head as to an old friend. The farmer sat down, and signified the young man was to do the same.

"Thank you, but I am not tired," returned Pitou; but the other insisted, and he gave way.

"Pitou, I sent for you to join me," said the farmer.

"And you see I have not kept you waiting," retorted the National Guards captain, with his own frank smile, showing all his thirty-two teeth.

"No. You must have guessed that something serious is afoot."

"I suspected as much. But, I say, friend Billet, I do not see anything of Mayor Bailly or General Lafayette."

"Bailly is a traitor, who nearly murdered the lot of us on the parade-ground."

"Yes, I know that, as I picked you up there, almost swimming in your own blood."

"And Lafayette is another traitor, who wanted to take away the king."

"I did not know that. Lafayette a traitor, eh? I never would have thought of that. And the king?"

"He is the biggest traitor of the lot, Pitou."

"I can not say I am surprised at that," said Pitou.

"He conspires with the foreigner, and wants to deliver France to the enemy. The Tuileries is the center of the conspiracy, and we have decided to take possession of the Tuileries. Do you understand this, Pitou?"

"Of course I understand. But, look here, Master Billet; we took the Bastile, and this will not be so hard a job."

"That's where you are out."

"What, more difficult, when the walls are not so high?"

"That's so; but they are better guarded. The Bastile had but a hundred old soldiers to guard it, while the palace has three or four thousand men; this is saying nothing of the Bastile having been carried by surprise, while the Tuileries folk must know we mean to attack, and will be on the lookout."

"They will defend it, will they?" queried Pitou.

"Yes," replied Billet—"all the more as the defense is trusted to Count Charny, they say."

"Indeed. He did leave Boursonnes with his lady by the post," observed Pitou. "Lor', is he a traitor, too?"

"No; he is an aristocrat, that is all. He has always been for the court, so that he is no traitor to the people; he never asked us to put any faith in him."

"So it looks as though we will have a tussle with Lord Charny?"

"It is likely, friend Ange."

"What a queer thing it is, neighbors clapper-clawing!"

"Yes—what is called civil war, Pitou; but you are not obliged to fight unless you like."

"Excuse me, farmer, but it suits me from the time when it is to your taste."

"But I should even like it better if you did not fight."

"Why did you send for me, Master Billet?"

"I sent for you to give you this paper," replied Billet, with his face clouding.

"What is this all about?"

"It is the draft of my will."

"Your will?" cried Pitou, laughing. "Hang me, if you look like a man about to die!"

"No; but I may be a man who will get killed," returned the revolutionist, pointing to his gun and cartridge-box hanging on the wall.

"That's a fact," said Ange Pitou; "we are all mortal."

"So that I have come to place my will in your hands as the sole legatee."

"No, I thank you. But you are only saying this for a joke?"

"I am telling you a fact."

"But it can not be. When a man has rightful heirs he can not give away his property to outsiders."

"You are wrong, Pitou; he can."

"Then he ought not."

"I have no heirs," replied Billet, with a dark cloud passing over his face.

"No heirs? How about heiresses, then? What do you call Miss Catherine?"

"I do not know anybody of that name, Pitou."

"Come, come, farmer, do not say such things; you make me sad."

"Pitou, from the time when something is mine, it is mine to give away; in the same way, should I die, what I leave to you will be yours, to deal with as you please, to be given away as freely."

"Ha! Good—yes," exclaimed the young man, who began to understand; "then, if anything bad happens to you—But how stupid I am; nothing bad could happen to you."

"You yourself said just now that we are all mortal."

"So I did; but—well, I do not know but that you are right. I take the will, Master Billet; but is it true that if I fall heir, I can do as I please with the property?"

"No doubt, since it will be yours. And, you understand, you are a sound patriot, Pitou; they will not stand you off from it, as they might folk who have connived with the aristocrats."

"It's a bargain," said Pitou, who was getting it into his brain; "I accept."

"Then that is all I have to say to you. Put the paper in your pocket and go to sleep."

"What for?"

"Because we shall have some work to do to-morrow—no, this day, for it is two in the morning."

"Are you going out, Master Billet?"

"Only as far as the river."

"You are sure you do not want me?"

"On the other hand, you would be in my way."

"I suppose I might have a bite and a sup, then?"

"Of course. I forgot to ask if you might not be hungry."

"Because you know I am always hungry," said Pitou, laughing.

"I need not tell you where the larder is."

"No, no, master; do not worry about me. But you are going to come back here?"

"I shall return."

"Or else tell me where we are to meet?"

"It is useless, for I shall be home in an hour."

Pitou went in search of the eatables with an appetite which in him, as in the case of the king, no events could alter, however serious they might be, while Billet proceeded to the water-side to do what we know.

He had hardly arrived on the spot before a pebble fell, followed by another, and some more, teaching him that what Petion apprehended had come to pass, and that he was a prisoner to the Royalists. So he had flown, according to his instructions, to the Assembly, which had claimed the mayor, as we have described.

Petion, liberated, had only to walk through the House to get back to the mayor's office, leaving his carriage in the Tuileries yard to represent him.

For his part, Billet went home, and found Ange finishing his supper.

"Any news?" asked he.

"Nothing, except that day is breaking and the sky is the color of blood."

CHAPTER XI. IN THE MORNING.

The early sunbeams shone on two horsemen riding at a walking pace along the deserted water-side by the Tuileries. They were Colonel Mandat and his aid.

At one A. M. he was summoned to the City Hall, and refused to go; but on the order being renewed more peremptorily at two, Attorney Roederer said to him:

"Mark, colonel, that under the law the commander of the National Guard is to obey the City Government."

He decided to go, ignorant of two things.

In the first place, forty-seven sections of the forty-eight had joined to the town rulers each three commissioners, with orders to work with the officials and "save the country." Mandat expected to see the old board as before, and not at all to behold a hundred and forty-one fresh faces. Again, he had no idea of the order from this same board to clear the New Bridge of cannon and vacate St. John's Arcade, an order so important that Danton and Manuel personally had superintended its execution.

Consequently, on reaching the Pont Neuf, Mandat was stupefied to find it utterly deserted. He stopped and sent his aid to scout. In ten minutes this officer returned with the word that he saw no guns or National Guards, while the neighborhood was as lonesome as the bridge.

Mandat continued his way, though he perhaps ought to have gone back to the palace; but men, like things, must wend whither their destiny impels.

Proportionably to his approach to the City Hall, he seemed to enter into liveliness. In the same way as the blood in some organizations leaves the extremities cold and pale on rushing back to fortify the heart, so all the movement and heat—the Revolution, in short—was around the City Hall, the seat of popular life, the heart of that great body, Paris.

He stopped to send his officer to the Arcade; but the National Guard had been withdrawn from there, too. He wanted to retrace his steps; but the crowd had packed in behind him, and he was carried, like a waif on the wave, up the Hall steps.

"Stay here," he said to his follower, "and if evil befalls me, run and tell them at the palace."

Mandat yielded to the mob, and was floated into the grand hall, where he met strange and stern faces. It was the insurrection complete, demanding an account of the conduct of this man, who had not only tried to crush it in its development, but to strangle it in its birth.

One of the members of the Commune, the dread body which was to stifle the Assembly and struggle with the Convention, advanced and in the general's name asked:

"By whose order did you double the palace guard?"

"The Mayor of Paris'."

"Show that order."

"I left it at the Tuileries, so that it might be carried out during my absence."

"Why did you order out the cannon?"

"Because I set the battalion on the march, and the field-pieces move with the regiment."

"Where is Petion?"

"He was at the palace when I last saw him."

"A prisoner?"

"No; he was strolling about the gardens."

The interrogation was interrupted here by a new member bringing an unsealed letter, of which he asked leave to make communication. Mandat had no need to do more than cast a glance on this note to acknowledge that he was lost; he recognized his own writing. It was his order to the commanding officer at St. John's Arcade, sent at one in the morning, for him to attack in the rear the mob making for the palace, while the battalion on New Bridge attacked it in flank. This order had fallen into the Commune's hands after the dismissal of the soldiers.

The examination was over; for what could be more damning than this letter in any admissions of the accused?

The council decided that Mandat should be imprisoned in the abbey. The tale goes that the chairman of the board, in saying, "Remove the prisoner," made a sweep of the hand, edge downward, like chopping with an ax. As the guillotine was not in use then, it must have been an arranged sign—perhaps by the Invisibles, whose Grand Copt had divined that instrument.

At all events, the result showed that the sign was taken to imply death.

Hardly had Mandat gone down three of the City Hall steps before a pistol-shot shattered his skull, at the very instant when his son ran toward him. Three years before, the same reception had met Flesselles.

Mandat was only wounded, but as he rose, he fell again with a score of pike-wounds. The boy held out his hands and wailed for his father, but none paid any heed to him. Presently, in the bloody ring, where bare arms plunged amid flashing pikes and swords, a head was seen to surge up, detached from the trunk.

The boy swooned.

The aid-de-camp galloped back to the Tuileries to report what he had witnessed.

The murderers went off in two gangs: one took the body to the river, to throw it in, the other carried the head through the streets.

This was going on at four in the morning.

Let us precede the aid to the Tuileries, and see what was happening.

Having confessed, and made easy about matters since his conscience was tranquilized, the king, unable to resist the cravings of nature, went to bed. But we must say that he lay down dressed.

On the alarm-bells ringing more loudly, and the roll of the drums beating the reveille, he was roused.

Colonel Chesnaye, to whom Mandat had left his powers, awoke the monarch to have him address the National Guards, and by his presence and some timely words revive their enthusiasm.

The king rose, but half awake, dull and staggering. He was wearing a powdered wig, and he had flattened all the side he had lain upon. The hairdresser could not be found, so he had to go out with the wig out of trim.

Notified that the king was going to show himself to the defenders, the queen ran out from the council hall where she was.

In contrast with the poor sovereign, whose dim sight sought no one's glance, whose mouth-muscles were flabby and palpitating with involuntary twitches, while his violet coat suggested he was wearing mourning for majesty, the queen was burning with fever, although pale. Her eyes were red, though dry.

She kept close to this phantom of monarchy, who came out in the day instead of midnight, with owlish, blinking eyes. She hoped to inspire him with her overflow of life, strength, and courage.

All went well enough while this exhibition was in the rooms, though the National Guards, mixed in with the noblemen, seeing their ruler close to this poor, flaccid, heavy man, who had so badly failed on a similar occasion at Varennes, wondered if this really was the monarch whose poetical legend the women and the priests were already beginning to weave.

This was not the one they had expected to see.

The aged Duke of Mailly—with one of those good intentions destined to be another paving-stone for down below—drew his rapier, and sinking down at the foot of the king, vowed in a quavering voice to die, he and the old nobility which he represented, for the grandson of Henry IV. Here were two blunders: the National Guards had no great sympathy for the old nobility, and they were not here to defend the descendant of Henry IV., but the constitutional king.

So, in reply to a few shouts of "Hail to the king!" cheers for the nation burst forth on all sides.

Something to make up for this coolness was sought. The king was urged to go down into the royal yard. Alas! the poor potentate had no will of his own. Disturbed at his meals, and cheated, with only one hour's sleep instead of seven, he was but an automaton, receiving impetus from outside its material nature.

Who gave this impetus? The queen, a woman of nerve, who had neither slept nor eaten.

Some unhappy characters fail in all they undertake, when circumstances are beyond their level. Instead of attracting dissenters, Louis XVI., in going up to them, seemed expressly made to show how little glamour majesty can lend a man who has no genius or strength of mind.

Here, as in the rooms, when the Royalists managed to get up a shout of "Long live the king!" an immense hurrah for the nation replied to them.

The Royalists being dull enough to persist, the patriots overwhelmed them with "No, no, no; no other ruler than the nation!"

And the king, almost supplicating, added: "Yes, my sons, the nation and the monarch make but one henceforward."

"Bring the prince," whispered Marie Antoinette to Princess Elizabeth; "perhaps the sight of a child may touch them."

While they were looking for the dauphin, the king continued the sad review. The bad idea struck him to appeal to the artillerists, who were mainly Republicans. If the king had the gift of speech-making, he might have forced the men to listen to him, though their belief led them astray, for it would have been a daring step, and it might have helped him to face the cannon; but there was nothing exhilarating in his words or gesture; he stammered.

The Royalists tried to cover his stammerings with the luckless hail of "Long live the king!" already twice a failure, and it nearly brought about a collision.

Some cannoniers left their places and rushed over to the king, threatening him with their fists, and saying:

"Do you think that we will shoot down our brothers to defend a traitor like you?"

The queen drew the king back.

"Here comes the dauphin!" called out voices. "Long live the hope of the realm!"

Nobody took up the cry. The poor boy had come in at the wrong time; as theatrical language says, he had missed his cue.

The king went back into the palace, a downright retreat—almost a flight. When he got to his private rooms he dropped, puffing and blowing, into an easy-chair.

Stopping by the door, the queen looked around for some support. She spied Charny standing up by the door of her own rooms, and she went over to him.

"Ah, all is lost!" she moaned.

"I am afraid so, my lady," replied the Life Guardsman.

"Can we not still flee?"

"It is too late."

"What is left for us to do, then?"

"We can but die," responded Charny, bowing.

The queen heaved a sigh, and went into her own rooms.

CHAPTER XII. THE FIRST MASSACRE.

Mandat had hardly been slain, before the Commune nominated Santerre as commanding general in his stead, and he ordered the drums to beat in all the town and the bells to be rung harder than ever in all the steeples. He sent out patrols to scour the ways, and particularly to scout around the Assembly.

Some twenty prowlers were made prisoners, of whom half escaped before morning, leaving eleven in the Feuillants' guard-house. In their midst was a dandified young gentleman in the National Guard uniform, the newness of which, the superiority of his weapons, and the elegance of his style, made them suspect he was an aristocrat. He was quite calm. He said that he went to the palace on an order, which he showed the examining committee of the Feuillants' ward. It ran:

> "The National Guard, bearer of this paper, will go to the palace to learn what the state of affairs is, and return to report to the Attorney-and-Syndic-General of the Department.
>
> (Signed)   "Boirie,
>
> "Leroulx,
>
> "Municipal Officers."

The order was plain enough, but it was thought that the signatures were forged, and it was sent to the City Hall by a messenger to have them verified.

This last arrest had brought a large crowd around the place, and some such voices as are always to be heard at popular gatherings yelled for the prisoner's death.

An official saw that this desire must not spread, and was making a speech, to which the mob was yielding, when the messenger came back from the Hall to say the order was genuine, and they ought to set at liberty the prisoner named Suleau.

At this name, a woman in the mob raised her head and uttered a scream of rage.

"Suleau?" she cried. "Suleau, the editor of the 'Acts of the Apostles' newspaper, one of the slayers of Liege independence? Let me at this Suleau! I call for the death of Suleau!"

The crowd parted to let this little, wiry woman go through. She wore a riding-habit of the national colors, and was carrying a sword in a cross-belt. She went up to the city official and forced him to give her the place on the stand. Her head was barely above the concourse, before they all roared:

"Bravo, Theroigne!"

Indeed, Theroigne was a most popular woman, so that Suleau had made a hit when he said she was the bride of Citizen Populus, as well as referring to her free-and-easy morals.

Besides, he had published at Brussels the "Alarm for Kings," and thus helped the Belgian outbreak, and to replace under the Austrian cane and the priestly miter a noble people wishing to be free and join France.

At this very epoch Theroigne was writing her memoirs, and had read the part about her arrest there to the Jacobin Club.

She claimed the death of the ten other prisoners along with Suleau.

Through the door he heard her ringing voice, amid applause. He called the captain of the guard to him, and asked to be turned loose to the mob, that by his sacrifice he might save his fellow-prisoners. They did not believe he meant it. They refused to open the door to him, and he tried to jump out of the window, but they pulled him back. They did not think that they would be handed over to the slaughterers in cold blood; they were mistaken.

Intimidated by the yells, Chairman Bonjour yielded to Theroigne's demand, and bid the National Guardsman stand aloof from resisting the popular will. They stepped aside, and the door was left free. The mob burst into the jail and grabbed the first prisoner to hand.

It was a priest, Bonyon, a playwright noted for his failures and his epigrams. He was a large-built man, and fought desperately with the butchers, who tore him from the arms of the commissioner who tried to save him; though he had no weapon but his naked fists, he laid out two or three of the ruffians. A bayonet pinned him to the wall, so that he expired without being able to hit with his last blows.

Two of the prisoners managed to escape in the scuffle.

The next to the priest was an old Royal Guardsman, whose defense was not less vigorous; his death was but the more cruel. A third was cut to pieces before Suleau's turn came.

"There is your Suleau," said a woman to Theroigne.

She did not know him by sight; she thought he was a priest, and scoffed at him as the Abbe Suleau. Like a wild cat, she sprung at his throat. He was young, brave, and lusty; with a fist blow he sent her ten paces off, shook off the men who had seized him, and wrenching a saber from a hand, felled a couple of the assassins.

Then commenced a horrible conflict. Gaining ground toward the door, Suleau cut himself three times free; but he was obliged to turn round to get the cursed door open, and in that instant twenty blades ran through his body. He fell at the feet of Theroigne, who had the cruel joy of inflicting his last wound.

Another escaped, another stoutly resisted, but the rest were butchered like sheep. All the bodies were dragged to Vendome Place, where their heads were struck off and set on poles for a march through the town.

Thus, before the action, blood was spilled in two places; on the City Hall steps and in Feuillants' yard. We shall presently see it flow in the Tuileries; the brook after the rain-drops, the river after the brook.

While this massacre was being perpetrated, about nine A. M., some eleven thousand National Guards, gathered by the alarm-bell of Barbaroux and the drum-beat of Santerre, marched down the St. Antoine ward and came out on the Strand. They wanted the order to assail the Tuileries.

Made to wait for an hour, two stories beguiled them: either concessions were hoped from the court, or the St. Marceau ward was not ready, and they could not fall on without them.

A thousand pikemen waxed restless; as ever, the worst armed wanted to begin the fray. They broke through the ranks of the Guard, saying that they were going to do without them and take the palace.

Some of the Marseilles Federals and a few French Guards—of the same regiments which had stormed the Bastile three years before—took the lead and were acclaimed as chiefs. These were the vanguard of the insurrection.

In the meanwhile, the aid who had seen Mandat murdered had raced back to the Tuileries; but it was not till after the king and the queen had returned from the fiasco of a review that he announced the ghastly news.

The sound of a disturbance mounted to the first floor and entered by the open windows.

The City and the National Guards and the artillerists—the patriots, in short—had taunted the grenadiers with being the king's tools, saying that they were bought up by the court; and as they were ignorant of their commander's murder by the mob, a grenadier shouted:

"It looks as though that shuffler Mandat had sent few aristocrats here."

Mandat's eldest son was in the Guards' ranks—we know where the other boy was, uselessly trying to defend his father on the City Hall steps. At this insult to his absent sire, the young man sprung out of the line with his sword flourished. Three or four gunners rushed to meet him. Weber, the queen's attendant, was among the St. Roch district grenadiers, dressed as a National Guardsman. He flew to the young man's help. The clash of steel was heard as the quarrel spread between the two parties.

Drawn to the window by the noise, the queen perceived her foster-brother, and she sent the king's valet to bring him to her.

Weber came up and told what was happening, whereupon she acquainted him with the death of Mandat.

The uproar went on beneath the windows.

"The cannoniers are leaving their pieces," said Weber, looking out; "they have no spikes, but they have driven balls home without powder, so that they are rendered useless!"

"What do you think of all this?"

"I think your majesty had better consult Syndic Roederer, who seems the most honest man in the palace."

Roederer was brought before the queen in her private apartment as the clock struck nine.

CHAPTER XIII. THE REPULSE.

At this point, Captain Durler, of the Switzers, went up to the king to get orders from him or the major-general. The latter perceived the good captain as he was looking for some usher to introduce him.

"What do you want, captain?" he inquired.

"You, my Lord Charny, as you are the garrison commander. I want the final orders, as the head of the insurrectionary column appears on the Carrousel."

"You are not to let them force their way through, the king having decided to die in the midst of us."

"Rely on us, major-general," briefly replied Captain Durler, going back to his men with this order, which was their death-sentence.

As he said, the van of the rebels was in sight. It was the thousand pikemen, at the head of whom marched some twenty Marseilles men and fifteen French Guardsmen; in the ranks of the latter gleamed the bullion epaulets of a National Guards captain. This young officer was Ange Pitou, who had been recommended by Billet, and was charged with a mission of which we shall hear more.

Behind these, at a quarter-mile distance, came a considerable body of National Guards and Federals, preceded by a twelve-gun battery.

When the garrison commandant's order was transmitted to them, the Swiss fell silently into line and resolutely stood, with cold and gloomy firmness.

Less severely disciplined, the National Guards took up their post more disorderly and noisily, but with equal resolution.

The nobles, badly marshaled, and armed with striking weapons only, as swords or short-range pistols, and aware that the combat would be to the death, saw the moment approach with feverish glee when they could grapple with their ancient adversary, the people, the eternal athlete always thrown, but growing the stronger during eight centuries.

While the besieged were taking places, knocking was heard at the royal court-yard gate, and many voices shouting: "A flag of truce!" Over the wall at this spot was seen a white handkerchief tied to the tip of a pike-staff.

Roederer was on his way to the king when he saw this at the gate and ordered it to be opened. The janitor did so, and then ran off as fast as he could. Roederer confronted the foremost of the revolutionists.

"My friends," said he, "you wanted the gates open to a flag of truce, and not to an army. Who wants to hold the parley?"

"I am your man," said Pitou, with his sweet voice and bland smile.

"Who are you?"

"Captain Ange Pitou, of the Haramont Federal Volunteers."

Roederer did not know who the Haramont Federals were, but he judged it not worth while to inquire when time was so precious.

"What are you wanting?"

"I want way through for myself and my friends."

Pitou's friends, who were in rags, brandished their pikes, and looked with their savage eyes like dangerous enemies indeed.

"What do you want to go through here for?"

"To go and surround the Assembly. We have twelve guns, but shall not use e'er a one if you do as we wish."

"What do you wish?"

"The dethronement of the king."

"This is a grave question, sir," observed Roederer.

"Very grave," replied Pitou, with his customary politeness.

101

"It calls for some debate."

"That is only fair," returned Ange. "It is going on ten o'clock, less the quarter," said he; "if we do not have an answer by ten as it strikes, we shall begin our striking, too."

"Meanwhile, I suppose you will let us shut the door?"

Pitou ordered his crowd back; and the door was closed; but through the momentarily open door the besiegers had caught a glimpse of the formidable preparations made to receive them.

As soon as the door was closed, Pitou's followers had a keen desire to keep on parleying.

Some were hoisted upon their comrades' shoulders, so that they could bestride the wall, where they began to chat with the National Guardsmen inside. These shook hands with them, and they were merry together as the quarter of an hour passed.

Then a man came from the palace with the word that they were to be let in.

The invaders believed that they had their request granted, and they flocked in as soon as the doors were opened, like men who had been kept waiting—all in a heap. They stuck their caps on their pikes and whooped "Hurrah for the nation!"—"Long live the National Guard!"—"The Swiss forever!"

The National Guard echoed the shout of the nation, but the Swiss kept a gloomy and sinister muteness.

The inrush only ceased when the intruders were up to the cannon muzzles, where they stopped to look around.

The main vestibule was crammed with Swiss, three deep; on each step was a rank, so that six could fire at once.

Some of the invaders, including Pitou, began to consider, although it was rather late to reflect.

But though seeing the danger, the mob did not think of running away; it tried to turn it by jesting with the soldiers. The Guards took the joking as it was made, but the Swiss looked glum, for something had happened five minutes before the insurrectionary column marched up.

In the quarrel between the Guards and the grenadiers over the insult to Mandat, the former had parted from the Royalist guards, and as they went off they said good-bye to the Swiss, whom they wanted to go away with them.

They said that they would receive in their own homes as brothers any of the Swiss who would come with them.

Two from the Waldenses—that is, French Swiss—replied to the appeal made in their own tongue, and took the French by the hand. At the same instant two shots were fired up at the palace windows, and bullets struck the deserters in the very arms of those who decoyed them away.

Excellent marksmen as chamois-hunters, the Swiss officers had nipped the mutiny thus in the bud. It is plain now why the other Swiss were mute.

The men who had rushed into the yard were such as always oddly run before all outbreaks. They were armed with new pikes and old fire-arms— that is, worse than unarmed.

The cannoniers had come over to their side, as well as the National Guards, and they wanted to induce the Switzers to do the same.

They did not notice that time was passing and that the quarter of an hour Pitou had given Roederer had doubled; it was now a quarter past ten. They were having a good time; why should they worry?

One tatterdemalion had not a sword or a pike, but a pruning-hook, and he said to his next neighbor:

"Suppose I were to fish for a Swiss?"

"Good idea! Try your luck," said the other.

So he hooked a Swiss by the belt and drew him toward him, the soldier resisting just enough to make out that he was dragged.

"I have got a bite," said the fisher for men.

"Then, haul him in, but go gently," said his mate.

The man with the hook drew softly indeed, and the guardsman was drawn out of the entrance into the yard, like a fish from the pond onto the bank. Up rose loud whoops and roars of laughter.

"Try for another," said the crowd.

The fisherman hooked another, and jerked him out like the first. And so it went on to the fourth and the fifth, and the whole regiment might have melted away but for the order, "Make ready—take aim!"

On seeing the muskets leveled with the regular sound and precise movement marking evolutions of regular troops, one of the assailants— there is always some crazy-head to give the signal for slaughter under such circumstances—fired a pistol at the palace windows.

During the short space separating "Make ready" and "Fire" in the command, Pitou guessed what was going to happen.

"Flat on your faces!" he shouted to his men; "down flat, or you are all dead men!"

Suiting the action to the word, he flung himself on the ground.

Before there was time for his advice to be generally followed, the word "Fire!" rang in the entrance-way, which was filled with a crashing noise and smoke, while a hail of lead was spit forth as from one huge blunderbuss.

The compact mass—for perhaps half the column had entered the yard— swayed like the wheat-field before the gust, then like the same cropped by the scythe, reeled and fell down. Hardly a third was left alive.

These few fled, passing under the fire from two lines of guns and the barracks firing at close range. The musketeers would have killed each other but for the thick screen of fugitives between.

This curtain was ripped in wide places; four hundred men were stretched on the ground pavement, three hundred slain outright.

The hundred, more or less badly injured, groaned and tried to rise, but falling, gave part of the field of corpses a movement like the ocean swell, frightful to behold.

But gradually all died out, and apart from a few obstinate fellows who persisted in living, all fell into immobility.

The fugitives scattered over the Carrousel Square, and flowed out on the water-side on one hand and on the street by the other, yelling, "Murder—help! we were drawn into a death-trap."

On the New Bridge, they fell in with the main body. The bulk was commanded by two men on horseback, closely attended by one on foot, who seemed to have a share in the command.

"Help, Citizen Santerre!" shouted the flyers, recognizing in one of the riders the big brewer of St. Antoine, by his colossal stature, for which his huge Flemish horse was but a pedestal in keeping; "help! they are slaughtering our brothers."

"Who are?" demanded the brewer-general.

"The Swiss—they shot us down while we were cheek by jowl with them, a-kissing them."

"What do you think of this?" asked Santerre of the second horseman.

"Vaith, me dink of dot miliary broverb which it say: 'De soldier ought to march to where he hear dot gun-firing going on,'" replied the other rider, who was a small, fair man, with his hair cropped short, speaking with a strong German accent. "Zubbose we go where de goons go off, eh?"

"Hi! you had a young officer with you," called out the leader on foot to one of the runaways; "I don't see anything of him."

"He was the first to be dropped, citizen representative; and the more's the pity, for he was a brave young chap."

"Yes, he was a brave young man," replied, with a slight loss of color, the man addressed as a member of the House, "and he shall be bravely avenged. On you go, Citizen Santerre!"

"I believe, my dear Billet," said the brewer, "that in such a pinch we must call experience into play as well as courage."

"As you like."

"In consequence, I propose to place the command in the hands of Citizen Westerman—a real general and a friend of Danton—offering to obey him like a common soldier."

"I do not care what you do if you will only march right straight ahead," said the farmer.

"Do you accept the command, Citizen Westerman?" asked Santerre.

"I do," said the Russian, laconically.

"In that case give your orders."

"Vorwarts!" shouted Westerman, and the immense column, only halted for a breathing-spell, resumed the route.

As its pioneers entered at the same time the Carrousel by all gates, eleven struck on the Tuileries clocks.

CHAPTER XIV. THE LAST OF THE CHARNYS.

When Roederer entered the queen's apartments behind Weber, that lady was seated by the fire-place, with her back to the door; but she turned round on hearing it open.

"Well, sir?" she asked, without being very pointed in her inquiry.

"The honor has been done me of a call," replied Roederer.

"Yes, sir; you are one of the principal magistrates of the town, and your presence here is a shield for royalty. I wish to ask you, therefore, whether we have most to hope or to fear?"

"Little to hope, madame, and everything to fear."

"The mob is really marching upon the palace?"

"The front of the column is in the Carrousel, parleying with the Swiss Guards."

"Parleying? but I gave the Swiss the express order to meet brute force with force. Are they disobeying?"

"Nay, madame; the Swiss will die at their posts."

"And we at ours. The same as the Swiss are soldiers at the service of kings, kings are the soldiers at the beck of royalty."

Roederer held his peace.

"Have I the misfortune to entertain an opinion not agreeing with yours, sir?" asked the queen.

"Madame, I have no opinion unless I am asked for it."

"I do ask for it, sir."

"Then I shall state with the frankness of a believer. My opinion is that the king is ruined if he stays in the Tuileries."

"But if we do not stay here, where shall we go?" cried the queen, rising in high alarm.

"At present, there is no longer but one place of shelter for the royal family," responded the attorney-syndic.

"Name it, sir."

"The National Assembly."

"What do you say, sir?" demanded the queen, snapping her eyes and questioning like one who had not understood.

He repeated what he had said.

"Do you believe, sir, that I would ask a favor of those fellows?"

He was silent again.

"If we must meet enemies, I like those better who attack us in the broad day and in front, than those who wish to destroy us in the dark and from behind."

"Well, madame, it is for you to decide; either go and meet the people, or beat a retreat into the Assembly Hall."

"Beat a retreat? Are we so deprived of defenders that we must retreat before we have tried the exchange of shots?"

"Perhaps you will take the report, before you come to a conclusion, of some competent authority who knows the forces you have to dispose of?"

"Weber, bring me one of the principal officers—Maillardet, or Chesnaye, or—" she stopped on the point of saying "the Count of Charny."

Weber went out.

"If your majesty were to step up to the window, you would be able to judge for yourself."

With visible repugnance the lady took the few steps to the window, and, parting the curtains, saw the Carrousel Square, and the royal yard as well, crowded with ragged men bearing pikes.

"Good God! what are those fellows doing in here?" she exclaimed.

"I told your majesty—they are parleying."

"But they have entered the inner yards?"

"I thought I had better gain the time somehow for your majesty to come to a resolution."

The door opened.

"Come, come," cried the queen, without knowing that it would be Charny who appeared.

"I am here, madame," he said.

"Oh, is it you? Then I have nothing to say, as you told me a while ago what you thought should be done."

"Then the gentleman thought that the only course was—" said Roederer.

"To die," returned the queen.

"You see that what I propose is preferable, madame."

"Oh! on my soul, I do not know whether it is or not," groaned the queen.

"What does the gentleman suggest?"

"To take the king under the wing of the House."

"That is not death, but shame," said Charny.

"You hear that, sir?" cried the lady.

"Come, come," said the lawyer; "may there not be some middle course?"

Weber stepped forward.

"I am of very little account," he said, "and I know that it is very bold of me to speak in such company; but my devotion may inspire me. Suppose that your majesty only requested a deputation to watch over the safety of the king?"

"Well, I will consent to that. Lord Charny, if you approve of this suggestion, will you pray submit it to the king?"

Charny bowed and went out.

"Follow the count, Weber, and bring me the king's answer."

Weber went out after the nobleman.

Charny's presence, cold, stern and devoted, was so cruel a reproach to her as a woman, if not as a sovereign, that she shuddered in it. Perhaps she had some terrible forewarning of what was to happen.

Weber came back to say that the king accepted the idea.

"Two gentlemen are going to take his majesty's request to the Assembly."

"But look what they are doing!" exclaimed the queen.

The besiegers were busy fishing for Switzers.

Roederer looked out; but he had not the time to see what was in progress before a pistol-shot was followed by the formidable discharge. The building shook as though smitten to its foundations.

The queen screamed and fell back a step, but returned to the window, drawn by curiosity.

"Oh, see, see!" she cried, with flaring eyes, "they fly! they are routed! Why did you say, that we had no resource but in the Assembly?"

"Will your majesty be good enough to come with me," said the official.

"See, see," continued the queen, "there go the Swiss, making a sortie, and pursuing them! Oh, the Carrousel is swept free! Victory, victory!"

"In pity for yourself, madame, follow me," persisted Roederer.

Returning to her senses, she went with the attorney-syndic to the Louvre gallery, where he learned the king was, and which suited his purpose.

The queen had not an idea of it.

The gallery was barricaded half down, and it was cut through at a third of the way, where a temporary bridge was thrown across the gap; the foot of a fugitive might send it down, and so prevent the pursuers following into the Tuileries.

The king was in a window recess with his captains and some courtiers, and he held a spy-glass in his hand.

The queen had no need for it as she ran to the balcony.

The army of the insurrection was approaching, long and dense, covering the whole of the wide street along the riverside, and extending as far as the eye could reach.

Over the New Bridge, the southern districts effected a junction with the others.

All the church-bells of the town were frenziedly swinging out the tocsin, while the big bell of Notre Dame Cathedral overawed all the metallic vibrations with its bronze boom.

A burning sun sparkled in myriad points from the steel of gun-barrels and lance-points.

Like the rumblings of a storm, cannon were heard rolling on the pavement.

"What now, madame?" said Roederer.

Some fifty persons had gathered round the king.

The queen cast a long look on the group to see how much devotion lingered. Then, mute, not knowing to whom to turn, the poor creature took up her son and showed him to the officers of the court and army and National Guard, no longer the sovereign asking the throne for her heir, but the mother suing for protection for her boy.

During this time, the king was speaking in a low voice with the Commune attorney, or rather, the latter was repeating what he had said to the queen.

Two very distinct groups formed around the two sovereigns. The king's was cold and grave, and was composed of counselors who appeared of Roederer's opinion. The queen's was ardent, numerous, and enthusiastic young military men, who waved their hats, flourished their swords, raised their hands to the dauphin, kissed the hem of the queen's robe, and swore to die for both of them.

Marie Antoinette found some hope in this enthusiasm.

The king's party melted into the queen's, and with his usual impassibility, the monarch found himself the center of the two commingled. His unconcern might be courage.

The queen snatched a pair of pistols from Colonel Maillardet.

"Come, sire," she cried; "this is the time for you to show yourself and die in the midst of your friends!"

This action had carried enthusiasm to its height, and everybody waited for the king's reply, with parted lips and breath held in suspense.

A young, brave, and handsome king, who had sprung forward with blazing eye and quivering lip, to rush with the pistols in hand into the thick of the fight, might have recalled fortune to his crown.

They waited and they hoped.

Taking the pistols from the queen's hands, the king returned them to the owner.

"Monsieur Roederer," he said, "you were observing that I had better go over to the House?"

"Such is my advice," answered the legal agent of the Commune, bowing.

"Come away, gentlemen; there is nothing more to be done here," said the king.

Uttering a sigh, the queen took up her son in her arms, and said to her ladies:

"Come, ladies, since it is the king's desire," which was as much as to say to the others, "Expect nothing more from me."

In the corridor where she would have to pass through, Mme. Campan was waiting. She whispered to her: "How I wish I dwelt in a tower by the sea!"

The abandoned attendants looked at each other and seemed to say, "Is this the monarch for whom we came here to die?"

Colonel Chesnaye understood this mute inquiry, for he answered:

"No, gentlemen, it was for royalty. The wearer of the crown is mortal, but the principle imperishable."

The queen's ladies were terrified. They looked like so many marble statues standing in the corners and along the lobbies.

At last the king condescended to remember those he was casting off. At the foot of the stairs, he halted.

"But what will befall all those I leave behind?" he inquired.

"Sire," replied Roederer, "it will be easy enough for them to follow you out. As they are in plain dress, they can slip out through the gardens."

"Alas," said the queen, seeing Count Charny waiting for her by the garden gate, with his drawn sword, "I would I had heeded you when you advised me to flee."

The queen's Life Guardsman did not respond, but he went up to the king, and said:

"Sire, will you please exchange hats, lest yours single out your majesty?"

"Oh, you are right, on account of the white feather," said Louis. "Thank you, my lord." And he took the count's hat instead of his own.

"Does the king run any risk in this crossing?" inquired the queen.

"You see, madame, that if so, I have done all I could to turn the danger aside from the threatened one."

"Is your majesty ready?" asked the Swiss captain charged to escort the king across the gardens.

The king advanced between two rows of Swiss, keeping step with him, till suddenly they heard loud shouting on the left.

The door near the Flora restaurant had been burst through by the mob, and they rushed in, knowing that the king was going to the Assembly.

The leader of the band carried a head on a pole as the ensign.

The Swiss captain ordered a halt and called his men to get their guns ready.

"My Lord Charny," said the queen, "if you see me on the point of falling into those ruffians' hands, you will kill me, will you not?"

"I can not promise you that, for I shall be dead before they touch you."

"Bless us," said the king; "this is the head of our poor Colonel Mandat. I know it again."

The band of assassins did not dare to come too near, but they overwhelmed the royal pair with insults. Five or six shots were fired, and two Swiss fell—one dead.

"Do not fire," said Charny; "or not one of us will reach the House alive."

"That is so," observed the captain; "carry arms."

The soldiers shouldered their guns and all continued crossing diagonally. The first heats of the year had yellowed the chestnut-trees, and dry leaves were strewing the earth. The little prince found some sport in heaping them up with his foot and kicking them on his sister's.

"The leaves are falling early this year," observed the king.

"Did not one of those men write that royalty will not outlast the fall of the leaf?" questioned the queen.

"Yes, my lady," replied Charny.

"What was the name of this cunning prophet?"

"Manuel."

A new obstacle rose in the path of the royal family: a numerous crowd of men and women, who were waiting with menacing gestures and brandished weapons on the steps and the terrace which had to be gone over to reach the riding-school.

The danger was the worse from the Swiss being unable to keep in rank. The captain tried in vain to get through, and he showed so much rage that Roederer cried:

"Be careful, sir—you will lead to the king being killed."

They had to halt, but a messenger was sent to the Assembly to plead that the king wanted asylum.

The House sent a deputation, at the sight of whom the mob's fury was redoubled.

Nothing was to be heard but these shouts yelled with wrath:

"Down with Veto!"—"Over with the Austrian!"—"Dethronement or death!"

Understanding that it was in particular their mother who was threatened, the two children huddled up to her. The little dauphin asked:

"Lord Charny, why do these naughty people want to hurt my mamma?"

A gigantic man, armed with a pike, and roaring louder than the rest, "Down with Veto—death to the Austrian!" kept trying to stab the king and the queen.

The Swiss escort had gradually been forced away, so that the royal family had by them only the six noblemen who had left the palace with them, Charny, and the Assembly deputation.

There were still some thirty paces to go in the thick crowd.

It was evident that the lives of the pair were aimed at, and chiefly the queen's.

The struggle began at the staircase foot.

"If you do not sheathe your sword," said Roederer, "I will answer for nothing."

Without uttering a word, Charny put up his sword.

The party was lifted by the press as a skiff is tossed in a gale by the waves, and drawn toward the Assembly. The king was obliged to push away a ruffian who stuck his fist in his face. The little dauphin, almost smothered, screamed and held out his hands for help.

A man dashed forward and snatched him out of his mother's arms.

"My Lord Charny, my son!" she shrieked; "in Heaven's name, save my boy!"

Charny took a couple of steps in chase of the fellow with the prince, but as soon as he unmasked the queen, two or three hands dragged her toward them, and one clutched the neckerchief on her bosom. She sent up a scream.

Charny forgot Roederer's advice, and his sword disappeared its full length in the body of the wretch who had dared to lay hands on the queen.

The gang howled with rage on seeing one of their number slain, and rushed all the more fiercely on the group.

Highest of all the women yelled: "Why don't you kill the Austrian?"— "Give her to us to have her throat slit!"—"Death to her—death!"

Twenty naked arms were stretched out to seize her. Maddened by grief, thinking nothing of her own danger, she never ceased to cry:

"My son—save my son!"

They touched the portals of the Assembly, but the mob doubled their efforts for fear their prey would escape.

Charny was so closely pressed that he could only ply the handle of his sword. Among the clinched and menacing fists, he saw one holding a pistol and trying to get a shot at the queen. He dropped his sword, grasped the pistol by both hands, wrenched it from the holder, and discharged it into the body of the nearest assailant. The man fell as though blasted by lightning.

Charny stooped in the gap to regain his rapier.

At this moment, the queen entered the Assembly vestibule in the retinue of the king.

Charny's sword was already in a hand that had struck at her.

He flew at the murderer, but at this the doors were slammed, and on the step he dropped, at the same time felled by an iron bar on his head and a spear right through his heart.

"As fell my brothers," he muttered. "My poor Andrea!"

The fate of the Charnys was accomplished with the last one, as in the case of Valence and Isidore. That of the queen, for whom their lives were laid down, was yet to be fulfilled.

At this time, a dreadful discharge of great guns announced that the besiegers and the garrison were hard at work.

CHAPTER XV. THE BLOOD-STAINS.

For a space, the Swiss might believe that they had dealt with an army and wiped it off the earth. They had slain nearly four hundred men in the royal yard, and almost two hundred in the Carrousel; seven guns were the spoils.

As far as they could see, no foes were in sight.

One small isolated battery, planted on the terrace of a house facing the Swiss guard-house, continued its fire without their being able to silence it. As they believed they had suppressed the insurrection, they were taking measures to finish with this battery at any cost, when they heard on the water-side the rolling of drums and the much more awful rolling of artillery over the stones.

This was the army which the king was watching through his spy-glass from the Louvre gallery.

At the same time the rumor spread that the king had quitted the palace and had taken refuge in the House of Representatives.

It is hard to tell the effect produced by this news, even on the most firm adherents.

The monarch, who had promised to die at his royal post, deserting it and passing over to the enemy, or at least surrendering without striking a blow!

Thereupon the National Guards regarded themselves as released from their oath, and almost all withdrew.

Several noblemen followed them, thinking it foolish to die for a cause which acknowledged itself lost.

Alone the Swiss remained, somber and silent, the slaves of discipline.

From the top of the Flora terrace and the Louvre gallery windows, could be seen coming those heroic working-men whom no army had ever resisted, and who had in one day brought low the Bastile, though it had been taking root during four centuries.

These assailants had their plan; believing the king in his castle, they sought to encompass him so as to take him in it.

The column on the left bank had orders to get in by the river gates; that coming down St. Honore Street to break in the Feuillants' gates, while the column on the right bank were to attack in front, led by Westerman, with Santerre and Billet under his orders.

The last suddenly poured in by all the small entrances on the Carrousel, singing the "It shall go on."

The Marseilles men were in the lead, dragging in their midst two four-pounders loaded with grape-shot.

About two hundred Swiss were ranged in order of battle on Carrousel Square.

Straight to them marched the insurgents, and as the Swiss leveled their muskets, they opened their ranks and fired the pieces.

The soldiers discharged their guns, but they immediately fell back to the palace, leaving some thirty dead and wounded on the pavement.

Thereupon, the rebels, headed by the Breton and Marseilles Federals, rushed on the Tuileries, capturing the two yards—the royal, in the center, where there were so many dead, and the princes', near the river and the Flora restaurant.

Billet had wished to fight where Pitou fell, with a hope that he might be only wounded, so that he might do him the good turn he owed for picking him up on the parade-ground.

So he was one of the first to enter the center court. Such was the reek of blood that one might believe one was in the shambles; it rose from the heap of corpses, visible as a smoke in some places.

This sight and stench exasperated the attackers, who hurled themselves on the palace.

Besides, they could not have hung back had they wished, for they were shoved ahead by the masses incessantly spouted forth by the narrow doors of the Carrousel.

But we hasten to say that, though the front of the pile resembled a frame of fire-works in a display, none had the idea of flight.

Nevertheless, once inside the central yard, the insurgents, like those in whose gore they slipped, were caught between two fires: that from the clock entrance and from the double row of barracks.

The first thing to do was stop the latter.

The Marseillais threw themselves at the buildings like mad dogs on a brasier, but they could not demolish a wall with hands; they called for picks and crows.

Billet asked for torpedoes. Westerman knew that his lieutenant had the right idea, and he had petards made. At the risk of having these cannon-cartridges fired in their hands, the Marseilles men carried them with the matches lighted and flung them into the apertures. The woodwork was soon set aflame by these grenades, and the defenders were obliged to take refuge under the stairs.

Here the fighting went on with steel to steel and shot for shot.

Suddenly Billet felt hands from behind seize him, and he wheeled round, thinking he had an enemy to grapple: but he uttered a cry of delight. It was Pitou; but he was pretty hard to identify, for he was smothered in blood from head to foot; but he was safe and sound and without a single wound.

When he saw the Swiss muskets leveled, he had called out for all to drop flat, and he had set the example.

But his followers had not time to act like him. Like a monstrous scythe, the fusillade had swept along at breast-high, and laid two thirds of the human field, another volley bending and breaking the remainder.

Pitou was literally buried beneath the swathe, and bathed by the warm and nauseating stream. Despite the profoundly disagreeable feeling, Pitou resolved not to make any move, while bathed in the blood of the bodies stifling him, and to wait for a favorable time to show tokens of life.

He had to wait for over an hour, and every minute seemed an hour. But he judged he had the right cue when he heard his side's shouts of victory, and Billet's voice, among the many, calling him.

Thereupon, like the Titan under the mountain, he shook off the mound of carcasses covering him, and ran to press Billet to his heart, on recognizing him, without thinking that he might soil his clothes, whichever way he took him.

A Swiss volley, which sent a dozen men to the ground, recalled them to the gravity of the situation.

Two thousand yards of buildings were burning on the sides of the central court. It was sultry weather, without the least breath; like a dome of lead the smoke of the fire and powder pressed on the combatants; the smoke filled up the palace entrances. Each window flamed, but the front was sheeted in smoke; no one could tell who delivered death or who received it.

Pitou and Billet, with the Marseillais at the fore, pushed through the vapor into the vestibule. Here they met a wall of bayonets—the Swiss.

The Swiss commenced their retreat, a heroic one, leaving a rank of dead on each step, and the battalion most slowly retiring.

Forty-eight dead were counted that evening on those stairs.

Suddenly the cry rang through the rooms and corridors:

"Order of the king—the Swiss will cease firing."

It was two in the afternoon.

The following had happened in the House to lead to the order proclaimed in the Tuileries; one with the double advantage of lessening the assailants' exasperation and covering the vanquished with honor.

As the doors were closing behind the queen, but still while she could catch a glimpse of the bars, bayonets, and pikes menacing Charny, she had screamed and held her hands out toward the opening; but dragged away by her companions, at the same time by her maternal instinct, she had to enter the Assembly Hall.

There she had the great relief afforded her of seeing her son seated on the speaker's desk; the man who had carried him there waved his red cap triumphantly over the boy's head and shouted gladly:

"I have saved the son of my master—long live the dauphin!"

But a sudden revulsion of feeling made Marie Antoinette recur to Charny.

"Gentlemen," she said, "one of my bravest officers, most devoted of followers, has been left outside the door, in danger of death. I beg succor for him."

Five or six members sprung away at the appeal.

The king, the queen, and the rest of the royal family, with their attendants, proceeded to the seats intended for the cabinet officers, and took places there.

The Assembly received them standing, not from etiquette, but the respect misfortune compelled.

Before sitting down, the king held up his hand to intimate that he wished to speak.

"I came here to prevent a great crime," he said, in the silence; "I thought I could not be in safety anywhere else."

"Sire," returned Vergniaud, who presided, "you may rely on the firmness of the National Assembly; its members are sworn to die in defending the people's rights and the constitutional authorities."

As the king was taking his seat, a frightful musketry discharge resounded at the doors. It was the National Guards firing, intermingled with the insurgents, from the Feuillants' terrace, on the Swiss officers and soldiers forming the royal escort.

An officer of the National Guard, probably out of his senses, ran in in alarm, and only stopped by the bar, cried: "The Swiss—the Swiss are coming—they have forced past us!"

For an instant the House believed that the Swiss had overcome the outbreak and were coming to recover their master; for at the time Louis XVI. was much more the king to the Swiss than to any others.

With one spontaneous movement the House rose, all of a mind, and the representatives, spectators, officials, and guards, raising their hands, shouted, "Come what may, we vow to live and die free men!"

In such an oath the royals could take no part, so they remained seated, as the shout passed like a whirlwind over their heads from three thousand mouths. The error did not last long, but it was sublime.

In another quarter of an hour the cry was: "The palace is overrun—the insurgents are coming here to take the king!"

Thereupon the same men who had sworn to die free in their hatred of royalty, rose with the same spontaneity to swear they would defend the king to the death. The Swiss captain, Durler, was summoned outside to lay down his arms.

"I serve the king and not the House," he said. "Where is the royal order?"

They brought him into the Assembly by force; he was black with powder and red with blood.

"Sire," he said, "they want me to lay down arms. Is it the king's order?"

"Yes," said Louis; "hand your weapons to the National Guard. I do not want such brave men to perish."

Durler lowered his head with a sigh, but he insisted on a written order. The king scribbled on a paper: "The king orders the Swiss to lay down their arms and return into barracks."

This was what voices were crying throughout the Tuileries, on the stairs, and in the rooms and halls. As this order restored some quiet to the House, the speaker rang his bell and called for the debating to be resumed.

A member rose and pointed out that an article of the Constitution forbade debates in the king's presence.

"Quite so," said the king; "but where are you going to put us?"

"Sire," said the speaker, "we can give you the room and box of the 'Logographe,' which is vacant owing to the sheet having ceased to appear."

The ushers hastened to show the party where to go, and they had to retrace some of the path they had used to enter.

"What is this on the floor?" asked the queen. "It looks like blood!"

The servants said nothing; for while the spots might be blood, they were ignorant where they came from.

Strange to say, the stains grew larger and nearer together as they approached the box. To spare her the sight, the king quickened the pace, and opening the box door himself, he bid her enter.

The queen sprung forward; but even as she set foot on the sill, she uttered a scream of horror and drew back, with her hands covering her eyes. The presence of the blood-spots was explained, for a dead body had been placed in the room.

It was her almost stepping upon this which had caused her to leap back.

"Bless us," said the king, "it is poor Count Charny's body!" in the same tone as he had said to the gory relic on the pike, "This is poor Mandat's head."

Indeed, the deputies had snatched the body from the cutthroats, and ordered it to be taken into the empty room, without the least idea that the royal family would be consigned to this room in the next ten minutes. It was now carried out and the guests installed. They talked of cleaning up, but the queen shook her head in opposition, and was the first to take a place over the blood-stains. No one noticed that she burst her shoe-laces and dabbled her foot in the red, still warm blood.

"Oh, Charny, Charny!" she murmured; "why does not my life-blood ooze out here to the last drop to mingle with yours unto all eternity?"

Three P. M. struck.

The last of her Life Guards was no more, for in and about her palace nearly a thousand nobles and Swiss had fallen.

CHAPTER XVI. THE WIDOW.

During the slaying of the last of his adherents, what was the monarch doing? Being hungry, he called for his dinner.

Bread and wine, cold fowl, and meat, and fruit were brought him. He set to eating as if he were at a hunting-party, without noticing how he was stared at.

Among the eyes fixed on him was a pair burning because tears would not come. They were the queen's. It seemed to her that she could stay there forever, with her feet in her beloved's blood, living like a flower on the grave, with no nourishment but such as death affords.

She had suffered much lately, but never so as to see the king eating, for the position of affairs was serious enough to take away a man's appetite.

The Assembly, rather than protect him, had need of protection for itself. It was threatened by a formidable multitude roaring for the dethronement, and they obeyed by a decree. It proposed a National Convention, the head of the executive power being temporarily suspended from his functions. The Civil List was not to be paid. The king and family were to remain with the Assembly until order was restored; then they were to be placed in the Luxembourg Palace. Vergniaud told the deposed sovereign that it was the only way to save his neck.

This decree was proclaimed by torch-light that night.

The lights at the Tuileries fell on the ghastly scenes of the searchers and the mourners among the dead. Three thousand five hundred insurgents—to omit two hundred thieves shot by the rioters—had perished. This supposes as many wounded at the least. As the tumbrels rolled with the corpses to the working quarters, a chorus of curses went up against the king, the queen, their foreign camerilla, the nobles who had counseled them. Some swore revenge, and they had it in the coming massacres; others took up weapons and ran to the palace to vent their spite on the dead Swiss; others again crowded round the Assembly and the abbey where were prisoners, shouting "Vengeance."

The Tuileries presented an awful sight: smoking and bloody, deserted by all except the military posts which watched lest, under pretense of finding their dead, pillagers robbed the poor royal residence with its broken doors and smashed windows.

The post under the great clock, the main stairs, was commanded by a young captain of the National Guard, who was no doubt inspired by deep pity by the disaster, if one might judge by the expression of his countenance as each cart-load of dead was removed.

But the dreadful events did not seem to affect him a whit more than they had the deposed king. For, about eleven at night, he was busy in satisfying a monstrous appetite at the expense of a quartern loaf held under his left arm, while his knife-armed right hand unceasingly sliced off hunks of goodly size, which he inserted into a mouth opening to suit the dimensions of the piece.

Leaning against a vestibule pillar, he was watching the silent procession go by, like shades of mothers, wives and daughters, in the glare of torches set up here and there; they were asking of the extinct crater for the remains of their dear ones.

Suddenly the young officer started at the sight of one veiled phantom.

"It is the Countess of Charny," he muttered.

The shadow passed without seeing or hearing him.

The captain beckoned to his lieutenant.

"Desire," he said to him, on coming up, "yonder goes a poor lady of Doctor Gilbert's acquaintance, who is no doubt looking for her husband among the dead. I think of following her, in case she should need help and advice. I leave the command to you; keep good guard for both of us."

"Hang me if Doctor Gilbert's acquaintance has not a deucedly aristocratic bearing," remarked Lieutenant Desire Maniquet.

"Because she is an aristocrat—she is a countess," replied the officer.

"Go along; I will look out."

The Countess of Charny had already turned the first corner of the stairs, when the captain, detaching himself from his men, began to follow her at the respectful distance of fifteen paces. He was not mistaken. Poor Andrea was looking for her husband, not with the anxious thrill of doubt, but with the dull conviction of despair.

When Charny had been aroused in the midst of his joy and happiness by the echo of deeds in Paris, he had come, pale but resolute, to say to his wife:

"Dear Andrea, the King of France runs the risk of his life, and needs all his defenders. What ought I do?"

"Go where duty calls you, my dear George," she had replied, "and die for the king if you must."

"But how about you?" he asked.

"Do not be uneasy about me," she said. "As I live but in you, God may allow that we shall die together."

That settled all between those great hearts; they did not exchange a word further. When the post-horses came to the door, they set out, and were in town in five hours.

That same evening, we have seen Charny present himself for duty in his naval uniform at the same time that Dr. Gilbert was going to send for him.

Since that hour we know that he never quitted the queen.

Andrea had remained alone, shut in, praying; for a space she entertained the idea of imitating her husband, and claiming her station beside the queen, as he had beside the king; but she had not the courage.

The day of the ninth passed for her in anguish, but without anything positive. At nine in the morning next day she heard the cannon; it is needless to say that each echo of the war-like thunder thrilled her to the inmost fiber of her heart. The firing died out about two o'clock.

Were the people defeated, or the victors? she questioned, and was told that the people had won the day.

What had become of Charny in this terrible fray? She was sure that he had taken a leading part. On making inquiries again, she was told that the Swiss were slain, but most of the noblemen had got away.

But the night passed without his coming. In August, night comes late.

Not till ten o'clock did Andrea lose hope, when she drew a veil over her face and went out.

All along the road she met clusters of women wringing their hands and bands of men howling for revenge. She passed among them, protected by the grief of one and the rage of the other; besides, they were man-hunting that night, and not for women.

The women of both parties were weeping.

Arriving on the Carrousel, Andrea heard the proclamation that the rulers were deposed and safe under the wing of the Assembly, which was all she understood.

Seeing some carts go by, she asked what they carried, and was told the dead from the palace yards. Only the dead were being removed; the turn of the wounded would come later.

She thought that Charny would have fallen at the door of the rooms of the king or the queen, so she entered the palace. It was at the moment when Pitou, commanding the main entrance as the captain, saw, and, recognizing her, followed.

It is not possible to give an idea of the devastation in the Tuileries.

Blood poured out of the rooms and spouted like cascades down the stairs. In some of the chambers the bodies yet lay.

Like the other searchers, Andrea took a torch and looked at body after body. Thus she made her way to the royal rooms. Pitou still followed her.

Here, as in the other rooms, she sought in vain; she paused, undecided whither to turn. Seeing her embarrassment, the soldier went up to her.

"Alas, I suspect what your ladyship is seeking!" he said.

"Captain Pitou?" Andrea exclaimed.

"At your service."

"Yes, yes, I have great need of you," she said. Going to him, she took both his hands, and continued: "Do you know what has become of the Count of Charny?"

"I do not, my lady; but I can help you to look for him."

"There is one person who can tell us whether he is dead or alive, and where he is in either case," observed Andrea.

"Who is that, my lady?" queried the peasant.

"The queen," muttered Andrea.

"Do you know where she is?" inquired Pitou.

"I believe she is in the House, and I have still the hope that my Lord Charny is with her."

"Why, yes, yes," said Pitou, snatching at the hope for the mourner's sake; "would you like to go into the House?"

"But they may refuse me admission."

"I'll undertake to get the doors to open."

"Come, then."

Andrea flung the flambeau from her at the risk of setting fire to the place, for what mattered the Tuileries to her in such desperation? so deep that she could not find tears.

From having lived in the palace as the queen's attendant, she knew all the ways, and she led them back by short cuts to the grand entrance where Maniquet was on the lookout.

130

"How is your countess getting on?" he inquired.

"She hopes to find her lord in the House, where we are going. As we may find him," he added, in a low voice, "but dead, send me four stout lads to the Feuillants' gate, whom I may rely on to defend the body of an aristocrat as well as though a good patriot's."

"All right; go ahead with your countess; I will send the men."

Andrea was waiting at the garden end, where a sentry was posted; but as that was done by Pitou, he naturally let his captain pass.

The palace gardens were lighted by lamps set mostly on the statue pedestals. As it was almost as warm as in the heat of the day, and the slight breeze barely ruffled the leaves, the lamp-flames rose straight, like spear-heads, and lighted up the corpses strewn under the trees.

But Andrea felt so convinced that she should find her husband where the queen had taken refuge, that she walked on, without looking to either right or left. Thus they reached the Feuillants' gate.

The royal family had been gone an hour, and were in the record office, for the time. To reach them, there were two obstacles to pass: the guards and the royal attendants.

Pitou, as commanding the Tuileries, had the password, and could therefore conduct the lady up to the line of gentlemen.

The former favorite of the queen had but to use her name to take the next step.

On entering the little room reserved for her, the queen had thrown herself on the bed, and bit the pillow amid sobs and tears.

Certainly, one who had lost a throne and liberty, and perhaps would lose her life, had lost enough for no one to chaffer about the degree of her despair, and not to seek behind her deep abasement if some keener sorrow still did not draw these tears from her eyes and sobs from her bosom.

Owing to the respect inspired by this supreme grief, she had been left

131

alone at the first.

She heard the room door open, but as it might be that from the king's, she did not turn; though she heard steps approaching her pillow, she did not lift her head from it.

But suddenly she sprung up, as though a serpent had stung her.

A well-known voice had simply uttered the single word, "Madame."

"Andrea?" cried Marie Antoinette, rising on her elbow. "What do you want?"

"I want the answer God demanded of Cain when He said, 'What have you done with your brother'?"

"With this difference," returned the queen, "That Cain had killed his brother; whereas I—so gladly—would give not only my existence, but ten lives, to save his dear one."

Andrea staggered; a cold sweat burst out on her forehead, and her teeth chattered.

"Then he was killed?" she faltered, making a great effort.

"Do you think I am wailing for my crown?" demanded the fallen majesty, looking hard at her. "Do you believe that if this blood were mine"— here she showed her dyed foot—"I should not have washed it off?"

Andrea became lividly pale.

"Then you know where his body is?" she said.

"I could take you to it, if I were allowed to go forth," said the prisoner.

Andrea went out at the door by which Pitou was waiting.

"Captain," she said, "one of my friends, a lady of the queen's, offers to take me where the count's body is. May she go out with me?"

"On condition that you bring her back whence she came," said the officer.

"That will do."

"Comrade," said Pitou to his sentry, "one of the queen's women wants to go out to help us find the body of a brave officer of whom this lady is the widow. I will answer for her with my head."

"That is good enough for me, captain," was the reply.

The anteroom door opened and the queen appeared, but she had a veil wound round her head. They went down the stairs, the queen leading.

After a twenty-seven hours' session, the House had adjourned, and the immense hall, where so much noise and so many events had been compressed, was dumb, void, and somber as a sepulcher.

The queen called for a light. Pitou picked up an extinguished link, lighted it at a lantern, and handed it to her, and she resumed the march. As they passed the entrance door, the queen pointed to it.

"He was killed there," she said.

Andrea did not reply; she seemed a specter haunting one who had called her up.

The queen lowered the torch to the floor in the lobby, saying: "Behold his blood."

Andrea remained mute.

The conductress went straight to a closet attached to the "Logographe" box, pulled the door open, and said, as she held up the light to illumine the interior:

"Here is his body."

Andrea entered the room, knelt down, and taking the head upon her knee, she said:

"Madame, I thank you; this is all I wanted of you."

"But I have something to ask you—won't you forgive me?"

There fell a short silence, as though Andrea were reflecting.

"Yes," she replied, at length, "for I shall be with him on the morrow."

The queen drew a pair of scissors from her bosom, where they were hidden like a weapon to be used in an extremity.

"Then would you kindly—" She spoke almost supplicatingly, as she held out the joined blades to the mourner.

Andrea cut a lock of hair from the corpse's brow, and handed it and the instrument to the other. She caught her hand and kissed it, but Andrea snatched away hers, as though the lips of her royal mistress had scorched her.

"Ah!" muttered the queen, throwing a last glance on the remains, "who can tell which of us loved him the most?"

"Oh, my darling George," retorted Andrea, in the same low tone, "I trust that you at least know now that I loved you the best!"

The queen went back on the way to her prison, leaving Andrea with the remains of her husband, on which a pale moonbeam fell through a small grated window, like the gaze of a friend.

Without knowing who she was, Pitou conducted Marie Antoinette, and saw her safely lodged. Relieved of his responsibility toward the soldier on guard, he went out on the terrace to see if the squad he had asked of Maniquet had arrived. The four were waiting.

"Come in," said Pitou.

Using the torch which he had taken from the queen's hands, he led his men to the room where Andrea was still gazing on her husband's white but still handsome face in the moonshine. The torch-light made her look up.

"What do you want?" she challenged of the Guards, as though she thought they came to rob her of the dead.

"My lady," said Pitou, "we come to carry the body of Count Charny to his house in Coq-Heron Street."

"Will you swear to me that it is purely for that?" Andrea asked.

Pitou held out his hand over the dead body with a dignity of which he might be believed incapable.

"Then I owe you apology, and I will pray God," said Andrea, "in my last moments, to spare you and yours such woe as He hath afflicted me with."

The four men took up the warrior on their muskets, and Pitou, with his drawn sword, placed himself at the head of the funeral party. Andrea walked beside the corpse, holding the cold and rigid hand in her own. They put the body on the countess's bed, when that lady said to the National Guardsmen:

"Receive the blessings of one who will pray to God for you to-morrow before Him. Captain Pitou," she added, "I owe you more than I ever can repay you. May I rely on you for a final service?"

"Order me, madame."

"Arrange that Doctor Gilbert shall be here at eight o'clock in the morning."

Pitou bowed and went out. Turning his head as he did so, he saw Andrea kneel at the bed as at an altar.

CHAPTER XVII. WHAT ANDREA WANTED OF GILBERT.

At eight precisely next day, Gilbert knocked at the house-door of the Countess of Charny.

On hearing of her request made to Pitou, he had asked him for full particulars of the occurrence, and he had pondered over them.

As he went out in the morning, he sent for Pitou to go to the college where his son and Andrea's, Sebastian, was being educated, and bring him to Coq-Heron Street. He was to wait at the door there for the physician to come out.

No doubt the old janitor had been informed of the doctor's visit, for he showed him at once into the sitting-room.

Andrea was waiting, clad in full mourning. It was clear that she had neither slept nor wept all the night through; her face was pale and her eyes dry. Never had the lines of her countenance, always indicative of willfulness carried to the degree of stubbornness, been more firmly fixed.

It was hard to tell what resolution that loving heart had settled on, but it was plain that it had come to one. This was comprehended by Gilbert at a first glance, as he was a skilled observer and a reasoning physician.

He bowed and waited.

"I asked you to come because I want a favor done, and it must be put to one who can not refuse it me."

"You are right, madame; not, perhaps, in what you are about to ask, but in what you have done; for you have the right to claim of me anything, even to my life."

She smiled bitterly.

"Your life, sir, is one of those so precious to mankind that I should be the first to pray God to prolong it and make it happy, far from wishing it abridged. But acknowledge that yours is placed under happy influences, as there are others seemingly doomed beneath a fatal star."

Gilbert was silent.

"Mine, for instance," went on Andrea; "what do you say about mine? Let me recall it briefly," she said, as Gilbert lowered his eyes. "I was born poor. My father was a ruined spendthrift before I was born. My childhood was sad and lonesome. You knew what my father was, as you were born on his estate and grew up in our house, and you can measure the little affection he had for me.

"Two persons, one of whom was bound to be a stranger to me, while the other was unknown, exercised a fatal and mysterious sway over me, in which my will went for naught. One disposed of my soul, the other of my body. I became a mother without ceasing to be a virgin. By this horrid event I nearly lost the love of the only being who ever loved me—my brother Philip.

"I took refuge in the idea of motherhood, and that my babe would love me; but it was snatched from me within an hour of its birth. I was therefore a wife without a husband, a mother without a child.

"A queen's friendship consoled me.

"One day chance sent me in a public vehicle with the queen and a handsome young gallant, whom fatality caused me to love, though I had never loved a soul.

"He fell in love with the queen. I became the confidante in this amour. As I believe you have loved without return, Doctor Gilbert, you can understand what I suffered. Yet this was not enough. It happened on a day that the queen came to me to say: 'Andrea, save my life; more than life—my honor!' It was necessary that I should become the bride of the man I had loved three years without becoming his wife. I agreed. Five years I dwelt beside that man, flame within, but ice without; a statue with a burning heart. Doctor, as a doctor, can you understand what my heart went through?

"One day—day of unspeakable bliss—my self-sacrifice, silence, and devotion touched that man. For six years I loved him without letting him suspect it by a look, when he came all of a quiver to throw himself at my feet and cry: 'I know all, and I love you!'

"Willing to recompense me, God, in giving me my husband, restored me my child. A year flew by like a day—nay, an hour, a minute. This year is all I call my life.

"Four days ago the lightning fell at my feet. The count's honor bid him go to Paris, to die there. I did not make any remark, did not shed a tear; I went with him. Hardly had we arrived before he parted from me. Last night I found him, slain. There he rests, in the next room.

"Do you think I am too ambitious to crave to lie in the same grave? Do you believe you can refuse the request I make to you?

"Doctor Gilbert, you are a learned physician and a skillful chemist. You have been guilty of great wrongs to me, and you have much to expiate as regards me. Well, give me a swift sure poison, and I shall not merely forgive you all, but die with a heart full of gratitude to you."

"Madame," replied Gilbert, "as you say, your life has been one long, dolorous trial, and for it all glory be yours, since you have borne it nobly and saintly, like a martyr."

She gave an impatient toss of the head, as if she wanted a direct answer.

"Now you say to your torturer: 'You made my life a misery; give me a sweet death.' You have the right to do this, and there is reason in your adding: 'You must do it, for you have no right to refuse me anything,' Do you still want the poison?"

"I entreat you to be friend enough to give it me."

"Is life so heavy to you that it is impossible for you to support it?"

"Death is the sweetest boon man can give me; the greatest blessing God may grant me."

"In ten minutes you shall have your wish, madame," responded Gilbert, bowing and taking a step toward the door.

"Ah!" said the lady, holding out her hand to him, "you do me more kindness in an instant than you did harm in all your life. God bless you, Gilbert!"

He hurried out. At the door he found Pitou and Sebastian, waiting in a hack.

"Sebastian," he said to the youth, drawing a small vial attached to a gold chain from inside his clothes at his breast, "take this flask of liquor to the Countess of Charny."

"How long am I to stay with her?"

"As long as you like."

"Where am I to find you?"

"I shall be waiting here."

Taking the small bottle, the young man went in-doors. In a quarter of an hour he came forth. Gilbert cast on him a rapid glance. He brought back the tiny flask untouched.

"What did she say?" asked Gilbert.

"'Not from your hand, my child!'"

"What did she do then?"

"She fell a-weeping."

"She is saved," said Gilbert. "Come, my boy," and he embraced him more tenderly than ever before. In clasping him to his heart, he heard the crackling of paper.

"What is that?" he asked, with a nervous laugh of joy. "Do you by chance carry your compositions in your breast-pocket?"

"There, I had forgotten," said the youth, taking a parchment from his pocket. "The countess gave it me, and says it is to be deposited in the proper registry."

The doctor examined the paper. It was a document which empowered, in default of heirs male, to the titles of Philip de Taverney, Knight of Redcastle, Sebastian Emile Gilbert, son of Andrea Taverney, Countess of Charny, to wear that title honorarily until the king should make it good to him by favor of his mother's service to the Crown, and perhaps award him the estates to maintain the dignity.

"Keep it," said Gilbert, with a melancholy smile; "as well date it from the Greek kalends! The king, I fear, will nevermore dispose of more than six-feet-by-three of landed property in his once kingdom of France."

Gilbert could jest, for he believed Andrea saved.

He had reckoned without Marat. A week after, he learned that the scoundrel had denounced the favorite of the queen, and that the widowed Countess of Charny had been arrested and lodged in the old Abbey Prison.

CHAPTER XVIII. THE ASSEMBLY AND THE COMMUNE.

It was the Commune which had caused the attack on the palace, which the king must have seen, for he took refuge in the House, and not in the City Hall. The Commune wanted to smother the wolf—the she-wolf and the whelps—between two blankets in their den.

This shelter to the royals converted the Assembly into Royalists. It was asserted that the Luxembourg Palace, assigned to the king as a residence, had a secret communication with those catacombs which burrow under Paris, so that he might get away at any hour.

The Assembly did not want to quarrel with the Commune over such a trifle, and allowed it to choose the royal house of detention.

The city pitched on the temple. It was not a palace, but a prison, under the town's hand; an old, lonely tower, strong, heavy, lugubrious. In it Philip the Fair broke up the Middle Ages revolting against him, and was royalty to be broken down in it now?

All the houses in the neighborhood were illuminated as the royal captives were taken hither to the part called "the palace," from Count Artois making it his city residence. They were happy to hold in bondage the king no more, but the friend of the foreign foe, the great enemy of the Revolution, and the ally of the nobles and the clergy.

The royal servants looked at the lodgings with stupefaction. In their tearful eyes were still the splendors of the kingly dwellings, while this was not even a prison into which was flung their master, but a kennel! Misfortune was not to have any majesty.

But, through strength of mind or dullness, the king remained unaffected, and slept on the poverty-stricken bed as tranquilly as in his palace, perhaps more so.

At this time, the king would have been the happiest man in the world had he been given a country cottage with ten acres, a forge, a chapel and a chaplain, and a library of travel-books, with his wife and children. But it was altogether different with the queen.

The proud lioness did not rage at the sight of her cage, but that was because so sharp a sorrow ached in her heart that she was blind and insensible to all around her.

The men who had done the fighting in the capture of the Royalist stronghold were willing that the prisoners, Swiss and gentlemen, should be tried by court-martial. But Marat shrieked for massacre, as making shorter work than even a drum-head court.

Danton yielded to him. Before the snake the lion was cowed, and slunk away, trying to act the fox.

The city wards pressed the Assembly to create an extraordinary tribunal. It was established on the twentieth, and condemned a Royalist to death. The execution took place by torch-light, with such horrible effect, that the executioner, in the act of holding up the lopped-off head to the mob, yelled and fell dead off upon the pavement.

The Revolution of 1789, with Necker, Bailly, and Sieyes, ended in 1790; that of Barnave, Lafayette, and Mirabeau in 1792, while the Red Revolution, the bloody one of Danton, Marat, and Robespierre, was commencing.

Lafayette, repulsed instinctively by the army, which he had called upon in an address to march on Paris and restore the king, had fled abroad.

Meanwhile, the Austrians, whom the queen had prayed to see in the moonlight from her palace windows, had captured Longwy. The other extremity of France, La Vendee, had risen on the eve of this surrender.

To meet this condition of affairs, the Assembly assigned Dumouriez to the command of the Army of the East; ordered the arrest of Lafayette; decreed the razing of Longwy when it should be retaken; banished all priests who would not take the oath of allegiance; authorized house-to-house visits for aristocrats and weapons, and sold all the property of fugitives.

The Commune, with Marat as its prophet, set up the guillotine on Carrousel Square, with an apology that it could only send one victim a day, owing to the trouble of obtaining convictions.

On the 28th of August, the Assembly passed the law on domiciliary visits. The rumor spread that the Austrian and Prussian armies had effected their junction, and that Longwy had fallen.

It followed that the enemy, so long prayed for by the king, the nobles, and the priests, was marching upon Paris, and might be here in six stages, if nothing stopped him.

What would happen then to this boiling crater from which the shocks had made the Old World quake the last three years?

The insolent jest of Bouille would be realized, that not one stone would be left upon another.

It was considered a sure thing that a general, terrible, and inexorable doom was to fall on the Parisians after their city was destroyed. A letter found in the Tuileries had said:

"In the rear of the army will travel the courts, informed on the journey by the fugitives of the misdeeds and their authors, so that no time will be lost in trying the Jacobins in the Prussian king's camp, and getting their halters ready."

The stories also came of the Uhlans seizing Republican local worthies and cropping their ears. If they acted thus on the threshold, what would they do when within the gates?

It was no longer a secret.

A great throne would be erected before the heap of ruins which was Paris. All the population would be dragged and beaten into passing before it; the good and the bad would be sifted apart as on the last judgment day. The good—in other words, the religious and the Royalists—would pass to the right, and France would be turned over to them for them to work their pleasure; the bad, the rebels, would be sent to the left, where would be waiting the guillotine, invented by the Revolution, which would perish by it.

But to face the foreign invader, had this poor people any self-support? Those whom they had worshiped, enriched, and paid to defend her, would they stand up for her now? No.

The king conspired with the enemy, and from the temple, where he was confined, continued to correspond with the Prussians and Austrians: the nobility marched against France, and were formed in battle array by her princes; her priests made the peasants revolt. From their prison cells, the Royalist prisoners cheered over the defeats of the French by the Prussians, and the Prussians at Longwy were hailed by the captives in the abbey and the temple.

In consequence, Danton, the man for extremes, rushed into the rostrum.

"When the country is in danger, everything belongs to the country," he said.

All the dwellings were searched, and three thousand persons arrested; two thousand guns were taken.

Terror was needed; they obtained it. The worst mischief from the search was one not foreseen; the mob had entered rich houses, and the sight of luxuries had redoubled their hatred, though not inciting them to pillage. There was so little robbery that Beaumarchais, then in jail, said that the crowd nearly drowned a woman who plucked a rose in his gardens.

On this general search day, the Commune summoned before its bar a Girondist editor, Girey-Dupre, who took refuge at the War Ministry, from not having time to get to the House. Insulted by one of its members, the Girondists summoned the Commune's president, Huguenin, before its bar for having allowed the Ministry to take Girey by force.

Huguenin would not come, and he was ordered to be arrested by main force, while a fresh election for a Commune was decreed.

The present one determined to hold office, and thus was civil war set going. No longer the mob against the king, citizens against aristocrats, the cottage against the castle; but hovels against houses, ward against ward, pike to pike, and mob to mob.

Marat called for the massacre of the Assembly; that was nothing, as people were used to his shrieks for wholesale slaughter. But Robespierre, the prudent, wary, vague, and double-meaning denunciator, came out boldly for all to fly to arms, not merely to defend, but to attack. He must have judged the Commune was very strong to do this.

The physician who might have his fingers on the pulse of France at this period must have felt the circulation run up at every beat.

The Assembly feared the working-men, who had broken in the Tuileries gates and might dash in the Assembly doors. It feared, too, that if it took up arms against the Commune, it would not only be abandoned by the Revolutionists, but be bolstered up by the moderate Royalists. In that case it would be utterly lost.

It was felt that any event, however slight, might lead this disturbance to colossal proportions. The event, related by one of our characters, who has dropped from sight for some time, and who took a share in it, occurred in the Chatelet Prison.

CHAPTER XIX. CAPTAIN BEAUSIRE APPEARS AGAIN.

After the capture of the Tuileries, a special court was instituted to try cases of theft committed at the palace. Two or three hundred thieves, caught red-handed, had been shot off-hand, but there were as many more who had contrived to hide their acts.

Among the number of these sly depredators was "Captain" Beausire, a corporal of the French Guards once on a time, but more conspicuous as a card-sharper and for his hand in the plot of robbers by which the court jewelers were nearly defrauded of the celebrated set of diamonds which we have written about under their historic name of "The Queen's Necklace."

This Beausire had entered the palace, but in the rear of the conquerors. He was too full of sense to be among the first where danger lay in taking the lead.

It was not his political opinions that carried him into the king's home, to weep over the fall of monarchy or to applaud the triumph of the people; bless your innocence, no! Captain Beausire came as a mere sight-seer, soaring above those human weaknesses known as opinions, and having but one aim in view, to wit, to ascertain whether those who lost a throne might not have lost at the same time some article of value rather more portable and easy to put out of sight.

To be in harmony with the situation, Beausire had clapped on an enormous red cap, was armed with the largest-sized saber, and had splashed his shirt-front and hands with blood from the first quite dead man he stumbled upon. Like the wolf skulking round the edge and the vulture hovering over the battle-field, perhaps taken for having helped in the slaughter, some believed he had been one of the vanquishers.

The most did so accept him as they heard him bellow "Death to the aristocrats!" and saw him poke under beds, dash open cupboards, and even bureau drawers, in order to make sure that no aristocrat had hidden there.

However, for the discomfiture of Captain Beausire, at this time, a man was present who did not peep under beds or open drawers, but who, having entered while the firing was hot, though he carried no arms with the conquerors, though he did no conquering, walked about with his hands behind his back, as he might have done in a public park on a holiday. Cold and calm in his threadbare but well-brushed black suit, he was content to raise his voice from time to time to say:

"Do not forget, citizens, that you are not to kill women and not to touch the jewels."

He did not seem to feel any right to censure those who were killing men and throwing the furniture out of the windows.

At the first glance he had distinguished that Captain Beausire was not one of the storming-parties.

The consequence was that, about half past nine, Pitou, who had the post of honor, as we know, guarding the main entrance, saw a sort of woe-begone and slender giant stalk toward him from the interior of the palace, who said to him with politeness, but also with firmness, as if his mission was to modify disorder with order and temper vengeance with justice:

"Captain, you will see a fellow swagger down the stairs presently, wearing a red cap, swinging a saber and making broad gestures. Arrest him and have your men search him, for he has picked up a case of diamonds."

"Yes, Master Maillard," replied Pitou, touching his cap.

"Aha! so you know me, my friend?" said the ex-usher of the Chatelet Prison.

"I rather think I do know you," exclaimed Pitou. "Don't you remember me, Master Maillard? We took the Bastile together."

"That's very likely."

"We also marched to Versailles together in October."

"I did go there at that time."

"Of course you did; and the proof is that you shielded the ladies who went to call on the queen, and you had a duel with a janitor who would not let you go in."

"Then, for old acquaintance' sake, you will do what I say, eh?"

"That, and anything else—all you order. You are a regular patriot, you are."

"I pride myself on it," replied Maillard, "and that is why I can not permit the name we bear to be sullied. Attention! this is our man."

In fact, at this time, Beausire stamped down the grand stairs, waving his large sword and shouting: "The nation forever!"

Pitou made a sign to Maniquet and another, who placed themselves at the door without any parade, and he went to wait for the sham rioter at the foot of the stairs.

With a glance, the suspicious character noticed the movements, and as they no doubt disquieted him, he stopped, and made a turn to go back, as if he had forgotten something.

"Beg pardon, citizen," said Pitou; "this is the way out."

"Oh, is it?"

"And as the order is to vacate the Tuileries, out you go, if you please."

Beausire lifted his head and continued his descent.

At the last step he touched his hand to his red cap, and in an emphasized military tone, said:

"I say, brother-officer, can a comrade go out or not?"

"You are going out," returned Pitou; "only, in the first place, you must submit to a little formality."

"Hem! what is it, my handsome captain?"

"You will have to be searched."

"Search a patriot, a capturer of the tyrants' den, a man who has been exterminating aristocrats?"

"That's the order; so, comrade, since you are a fellow-soldier," said the National Guardsman, "stick your big toad-sticker in its sheath, now that all the aristos are slain, and let the search be done in good part, or, if not, I shall be driven to employ force."

"Force?" said Beausire. "Ha! you talk in this strain because you have twenty men at your back, my pretty captain; but if you and I were alone together—"

"If we were alone together, citizen," returned the man from the country, "I'd show you what I should do. In this way, I should seize your left wrist with my right hand; with my left, I should wrench your saber from your grasp, like this, and I should snap it under my foot, just like this, as being no longer worthy of handling by an honest man after a thief."

Putting into practice the theory he announced, Pitou disarmed the sham patriot, and breaking the sword, tossed the hilt afar.

"A thief? I, Captain de Beausire, a thief?" thundered the conqueror in the red cap.

"Search Captain Beausire with the de," said Pitou, pushing the card-sharper into the midst of his men.

"Well, go ahead with your search," replied the victim of suspicion, meekly dropping his arms.

They had not needed his permission to proceed with the ferreting; but to the great astonishment of Pitou, and especially of Maillard, all their searching was in vain. Whether they turned the pockets inside out, or examined the hems and linings, all they found on the ex-corporal was a pack of playing-cards so old that the faces were hardly to be told from the backs, as well as the sum of eleven cents.

Pitou looked at Maillard, who shrugged his shoulders as much as to say, "I have missed it somehow, but I do not know what I can do about it now."

"Go through him again," said Pitou, one of whose principal traits was patience.

They tried it again, but the second search was as unfruitful as the former; they only found the same pack of cards and eleven cents.

"Well," taunted Beausire, triumphantly, "is a sword still disgraced by having been handled by me?"

"No," replied Pitou; "and to prove it, if you are not satisfied with the excuses I tender you, one of my men shall lend you his, and I will give you any other satisfaction you may like."

"Thanks, no, young sir," said the other, drawing himself up to his full height; "you acted under orders, and an old veteran like me knows that an order is sacred. Now I beg to remark that Madame de Beausire must be anxious about my long absence, and if I am allowed to retire—"

"Go, sir," responded Pitou; "you are free."

Beausire saluted in a free-and-easy style and took himself out of the palace. Pitou looked round for Maillard, but he was not by.

"I fancy I saw him go up the stairs," said one of the Haramont men.

"You saw clearly, for he is coming down," observed Pitou.

Maillard was in fact descending, and as his long legs took the steps two by two, he was soon on the landing.

"Well, did you find anything?" he inquired.

"No," rejoined the captain.

"Then, I have been luckier than you, for I lighted on the case."

"So we were wrong, eh?"

"No; we were right."

Maillard opened the case and showed the old setting from which had been prized all the stones.

150

"Why, what does this mean?" Pitou wanted to know.

"That the scamp guessed what might happen, picked out the diamonds, and as he thought the setting would be in his way, he threw it with the case into the closet where I found it."

"That's clear enough. But what has become of the stones?"

"He found some means of juggling them away."

"The trickster!"

"Has he been long gone?" inquired Maillard.

"As you came down, he was passing through the middle yard."

"Which way did he take?"

"He went toward the water-side."

"Good-bye, captain."

"Are you going after him, Master Maillard?"

"I want to make a thorough job of it," returned the ex-usher.

And unfolding his long legs like a pair of compasses, he set off in pursuit of Captain Beausire.

Pitou was thinking the matter over when he recognized the Countess of Charny, and the events occurred which we have related in their proper time and place. Not to mix them up with this present matter, we think, falls into line here.

CHAPTER XX. THE EMETIC.

Rapid as was Maillard's gait, he could not catch up with his quarry, who had three things in his favor, namely: ten minutes' start, the darkness, and the number of passengers on the Carrousel, in the thick of whom he disappeared.

But when he got out upon the Tuileries quay, the ex-usher kept on, for he lived in the working-quarter, and it was not out of his way home to keep to the water-side.

A great concourse was upon the bridges, flocking to the open space before the Palace of Justice, where the dead were laid out for identification, and people sought for their dear ones, with hope, or, rather, fear.

Maillard followed the crowd.

At a corner there he had a friend in a druggist, or apothecary, as they said in those days. He dropped in there, sat down, and chatted of what had gone on, while the surgeons rushed in and about to get the materials they wanted for the injured; for among the corpses a moan, a scream, or palpable breathing showed that some wretch still lived, and he was hauled out and carried to the great hospital, after rough dressing.

So there was a great hubbub in the worthy chemist's store; but Maillard was not in the way; on such occasions they were delighted to see a patriot of the degree of a hero of the Bastile, who was balm itself to the lovers of liberty.

He had been there upward of a quarter of an hour, with his long legs tucked well under him and taking up as little room as possible, when a woman, of the age of thirty-eight or so, came in. Under the garb of most abject poverty, she preserved a vestige of former opulence, and a bearing of studied aristocracy, if not natural.

But what particularly struck Maillard was her marked likeness to the queen; he would have cried out with amaze but for his having great presence of mind. She held a little boy by the hand, and came up to the counter with an odd timidity, veiling the wretchedness of her garments as much as she could, though that was the more manifest from her taking extreme care of her face and her hands.

For some time it was impossible for her to make herself heard owing to the uproar; but at last she addressed the master of the establishment, saying:

"Please, sir, I want an emetic for my husband, who is ill."

"What sort do you want, citizeness?" asked the dispenser of drugs.

"Any sort, as long as it does not cost more than eleven cents."

This exact amount struck Maillard, for it will be remembered that eleven coppers were the findings in Beausire's pockets.

"Why should it not cost more than that?" inquired the chemist.

"Because that is all the small change my man could give me."

"Put up some tartar emetic," said the apothecary to an assistant, "and give it to the citizeness."

He turned to attend to other demands while the assistant made up the powder. But Maillard, who had nothing to do to distract his attention, concentrated all his wits on the woman who had but eleven cents.

"There you are, citizeness; here's your physic," said the drug clerk.

"Now, then, Toussaint," said the woman, with a drawl habitual to her, "give the gentleman the eleven cents, my boy."

"There it is," replied the boy, putting the pile of coppers on the counter. "Come home quick, Mamma Oliva, for papa is waiting."

He tried to drag her away, repeating, "Why don't you come quick? Papa is in such a hurry."

"Hi! hold on, citizeness!" cried the budding druggist; "you have only given me nine cents."

"What do you mean by only nine?" exclaimed the woman.

"Why, look here; you can reckon for yourself."

The woman did so, and saw there were just nine.

"What have you done with the other two coins, you wicked boy?" she asked.

"Me not know nothing about 'em," whimpered the child. "Do come home, Mamma Oliva!"

"You must know, for I let you carry the money."

"I must have lost 'em. But come along home," whined the boy.

"You have a bewitching little fellow there, citizeness," remarked Maillard; "he appears sharp-witted, but you will have to take care lest he become a thief."

"How dare you, sir!—a thief?" cried the woman called Oliva. "Why do you say such a thing, I should like to know?"

"Only because he has not lost the two cents, but hid them in his shoe."

"Me?" retorted the boy. "What a lie!"

"In the left shoe, citizeness—in the left," said Maillard.

In spite of the yell of young Toussaint, Mme. Oliva took off his left shoe and found the coppers in it. She handed them to the apothecary's clerk, and dragged away the urchin with threats of punishment which would have appeared terrible to the by-standers, if they had not been accompanied by soft words which no doubt sprung from maternal affection. Unimportant as the incident was in itself, it certainly would have passed without comment amid the surrounding grave circumstances, if the resemblance of the heroine to the queen had not impressed the witness. The result of his pondering over this was that he went up to his friend in drugs, and said to him, in a respite from trade:

"Did you not notice the likeness of that woman who just went out to—"

"The queen?" said the other, laughing.

"Yes; so you remarked it the same as I?"

"Oh, ever so long ago. It is a matter of history."

"I do not understand."

"Do you not remember the celebrated trial of 'The Queen's Necklace'?"

"Oh, you must not put such a question to an usher of the law courts—he could not forget that."

"Well, you must recall one Nicole Legay, alias Oliva."

"Oh, of course; you are right. She played herself as the queen upon the Prince Cardinal Rohan."

"While she was living with a discharged soldier, a bully and card-cheat, a spy and recruiter, named Beausire."

"What do you say?" broke out Maillard, as though snake-bitten.

"A rogue named Beausire," repeated the druggist.

"Is it he whom she styles her husband?" asked Maillard.

"Yes."

"And for whom she came to get the physic?"

"The rascal has been drinking too hard."

"An emetic?" continued Maillard, as one on the track of an important secret and did not wish to be turned astray.

"A vomitory—yes."

"By Jupiter, I have nailed my man!" exclaimed the visitor.

"What man?"

"The man who had only eleven cents—Captain de Beausire, in short. That is, if I knew where he lives."

"Well, I know if you do not; it is close by, No. 6 Juiverie Street."

"Then I am not astonished at young Beausire stealing two cents from his mother, for he is the son of the cheat."

"No cheat there—his living likeness."

"A chip of the old block. My dear friend," continued Maillard, "straight as a die, how long does your dose take to operate?"

"Immediately after taking; but these fellows fight shy of medicine. He will play fast and loose before he takes it, and his wife will have to make a cup of soup to wash the taste out of his mouth."

"You mean I may have time to do what I have to do?"

"I hope so; you seem to feel great interest in our Captain Beausire?"

"So much so that, for fear he will be very bad, I am going to get a couple of male nurses for him."

Leaving the drug store with a silent laugh, the only one he indulged in, Maillard hurried back to the Tuileries.

Pitou was absent, for we know he was attending on the Countess of Charny, but Lieutenant Maniquet was guarding the post. They recognized each other.

"Well, Citizen Maillard, did you overtake the fellow?" asked Maniquet.

"No; but I am on his track."

"Faith, it is a blessing; for though we did not find the diamonds on the knave, somehow I am ready to bet that he has them."

"Make the bet, citizen, and you will win," said the usher.

"Good; and can we help you catch him?"

"You can."

"In what way, Citizen Maillard? We are under your orders."

"I want a couple of honest men."

"You can take at random, then. Boulanger and Molicar, step out this way."

That was all the usher desired; and with the two soldiers of Haramont he proceeded at the double-quick to the residence of Beausire.

In the house they were guided by the cries of young Toussaint, still suffering from a correction, not maternal, as Papa Beausire, on account of the gravity of the misdemeanor, had deemed it his duty to intervene and add some cuffs from his hard hand to the gentle slap which Oliva had administered much against her will with her softer one to her beloved offspring.

The door was locked.

"In the name of the law, open!" called out Maillard.

A conversation in a low voice ensued, during which young Toussaint was hushed, as he thought that the abstraction of the two cents from his mother was a heinous crime for which Justice had risen in her wrath; while Beausire, who attributed it to the domiciliary visits, tried to tranquilize Oliva, though he was not wholly at his ease. He had, moreover, gulped down the tartar as soon as he had chastised his son.

Mme. Beausire had to take her course, and she opened the door just as Maillard was going to knock for a second time.

The three men entered, to the great terror of Oliva and Master Toussaint, who ran to hide under a ragged straw-bottomed chair.

Beausire had thrown himself on the bed, and Maillard had the satisfaction of seeing by the light of a cheap candle smoking in an iron holder that the physic paper was flat and empty on the night-table. The potion was swallowed, and they had only to abide the effects.

On the march, Maillard had related to the volunteers what had happened, so that they were fully cognizant of the state of matters.

"Citizens," he restricted himself to saying, "Captain Beausire is exactly like that princess in the Arabian Nights' Entertainment, who never spoke unless compelled, but who, whenever she opened her mouth, let fall a diamond. Do not, therefore, let Beausire spit out a word unless learning what it contains. I will wait for you at the Municipality offices. When the gentleman has nothing more to say to you, take him to the Chatelet Prison, where you will say Citizen Maillard sent him for safe keeping, and you will join me at the City Hall with what he shall have delivered."

The National Guards nodded in token of passive obedience, and placed themselves with Beausire between them. The apothecary had given good measure for eleven cents, and the effect of the emetic was most satisfactory.

About three in the morning, Maillard saw his two soldiers coming to him. They brought a hundred thousand francs' worth of diamonds of the purest water, wrapped in a copy of the prison register, stating that Beausire was under ward and lock. In his name and the two Haramontese, Maillard placed the gems in charge of the Commune attorney, who gave them a certificate that they had deserved the thanks of the country.

CHAPTER XXI. BEAUSIRE'S BRAVADO.

Imprisoned in the Chatelet, Beausire was brought before the jury specially charged to deal with thefts committed in the taking of the Tuileries. He could not deny what was only too clearly brought forth, so he most humbly confessed his deed and sued for clemency.

His antecedents being looked up, they so little edified the court on his moral character, that he was condemned to five years in the hulks and transportation to the plantations.

In vain did he allege that he had been led into crime by the most commendable feelings, namely, to provide a peaceful future for his wife and child; nothing could alter the doom, and as the court was one without appeal, and the sentences active, it was likely to be executed immediately.

Better for him had it not been deferred for a day. Fate would have it that one of his old associates was put in prison with him on the eve of his sentence being carried out. They renewed acquaintance and exchanged confidences.

The new-comer was, he said, concerned in a well-matured plot which was to burst on Strand Place or before the Justice Hall. The conspirators were to gather in a considerable number, as if to see the executions taking place at either spot, and, raising shouts of "Long live the king!" "The Prussians are coming, hurrah!" "Death to the nation!" they were to storm the City Hall, call to their help the National Guards, two thirds Royalist, or at least Constitutional, maintain the abolition of the Commune, and, in short, accomplish the loyal counter-revolution.

The mischief was that Beausire's old partner was the very man who was to give the signal. The others in the plot, ignorant of his arrest, would hie to the place of execution, and the rising would fall to the ground from nobody being there to start the cries.

This was the more lamentable, added the friend, from there never being a better arranged plot, and one that promised a more certain result.

His arrest was the more regrettable still as, in the turmoil, the prisoner would most certainly be rescued and get away, so that he would elude the branding-iron and the galleys.

Though Captain Beausire had no settled opinions, he leaned toward royalty, so he began to deplore the check to the scheme, in the first place for the king's sake, and then for his own.

All at once he struck his brow, for he was illumined with a bright idea.

"Why, this first execution is to be mine!" he said.

"Of course, and it would have been a rich streak of luck for you."

"But you say that it will not matter who gives the cue, for the plot will burst out?"

"Yes. But who will do this, when I am caged, and can not communicate with the lads outside?"

"I," replied Beausire in lofty, tragic tones. "Will I not be on the spot, since it is I whom they are to put in the pillory? So I am the man who will cry out the arranged shouts; it is not so very hard a task, methinks."

"I always said you were a genius," remarked the captain's friend, after being wonder-struck.

Beausire bowed.

"If you do this," continued the Royalist plotter, "you will not only be delivered and pardoned, but still further, when I proclaim that the success of the outbreak is due to you, you can shake hands with yourself beforehand on the great reward you will earn."

"I am not going to do the deed for anything like lucre," said the adventurer, with the most disinterested of manners.

"We all know that," rejoined the friend; "but when the reward comes along, I advise you not to refuse it."

"Oh, if you think I ought to take it—" faltered the gambler.

"I press you to, and if I had any power over you, I should order you," resumed the companion, majestically.

"I give in," said Beausire.

"Well, to-morrow we will breakfast together, for the governor of the jail will not refuse this favor to two old 'pals,' and we will crack a jolly good bottle of the rosy to the success of this plot."

Though Beausire may have had his doubts on the kindness of prison governors, the request was granted, to his great satisfaction. It was not one bottle they drained, but several. At the fourth, Beausire was a red-hot Royalist. Luckily, the warders came to take him to the Strand before he emptied the fifth. He stepped into the cart as into a triumphal chariot, disdainfully surveying the throng for whom he was storing up such a startling surprise.

On Notre Dame Bridge, a woman and a little boy were waiting for him to come along. He recognized poor Oliva, in tears, and young Toussaint, who, on beholding his father among the soldiers, said:

"Serves him right; what did he beat me for?"

The proud father smiled protectingly, and would have waved a blessing but his hands were tied behind his back.

The City Hall Square was crammed with people. They knew that this felon had robbed in the palace, and they had no pity for him. Hence, the Guards had their work cut out to keep them back when the cart stopped at the pillory foot.

Beausire looked on at the uproar and scuffling, as much as to say: "You shall see some fun in awhile; this is nothing to the joker I have up my sleeve!"

When he appeared on the pillory platform, there was general hooting; but at the supreme moment, when the executioner opened the culprit's shirt and pulled down the sleeve to bare the shoulder, and then stooped down to take the red-hot brand, that happened which always does—all was silent before the majesty of the law.

Beausire snatched at this lull, and gathering all his powers, he shouted in a full, ringing and sonorous voice:

"Long live the king! Hurrah for the Prussians! Down with the nation!"

However great a tumult the prisoner may have expected, the one this raised much exceeded it; the protest was not in shouts, but howls. The whole gathering uttered an immense roar and rushed on the pillory.

This time the guards were insufficient to protect their man. Their ranks were broken, the scaffold swarmed upon, the executioner thrown over, and the condemned one torn from the stand and flung into the surging mob.

He would have been flayed, dismembered, and torn to pieces but for one man, arrayed in his scarf as a town officer, who luckily saw it all from the City Hall steps.

It was the Commune attorney, Manuel. He had strongly humane feelings, which he often had to keep hidden, but they moved him at such times.

With great difficulty he fought his way to Beausire, and laying hold of him, said in a loud voice:

"In the name of the law, I claim this man!"

There was hesitation; he unloosed his scarf, floating it like a flag, and called for all good citizens to assist him.

A score clustered round him and drew Beausire, half dead, from the crowd. Manuel had him carried into the Hall, which was seriously threatened, so deep was the exasperation. Manuel came out on the balcony.

"This man is guilty," he said, "but of a crime for which he has not been tried. Let us select a jury from among us to assemble in a room of the City Hall. Whatever the sentence, it shall be executed; but let us have a legal sentence."

Is it not curious that such language should be used on the eve of the massacre of the prisoners, by one of the men accused of having organized it, at the peril of his life?

This pledge appeased the mob. Beausire was dragged before the improvised jury. He tried to defend himself, but his second crime was as patent as the first; only in the popular eye it was much graver.

Was it not a dreadful crime and deserving of condign punishment to cheer the king who was put in prison as a traitor, to hurrah for the Prussians who had captured a French town, and to wish death to the nation, in agony on a bed of pain?

So the jury decided not only that the culprit deserved the capital penalty, but that to mark the shame which the law had sought to define by substituting the guillotine for the gallows, that he should be hanged, and on the spot where he committed the offense.

Consequently the headsman of Paris had his orders to erect a gibbet on the pillory stand.

The view of this work and the certainty that the prisoner could not escape them, pacified the multitude.

This was the matter which the Assembly was busied with. It saw that everything tended to a massacre—a means of spreading terror and perpetuating the Commune. The end was that they voted that the Commune had acted to merit the gratitude of the country, and Robespierre, after praising it, asserted that the House had lost the public confidence, and that the only way for the people to save themselves was to retake their powers.

So the masses were to be without check, but with a heart full of vengeance, and charged to continue the August massacre of those who had fought for the palace on the tenth, by following them into the prisons.

It was the first of September, and a storm seemed to oppress everybody with its suspended lightning.

CHAPTER XXII. SET UPON DYING.

Thus stood matters, when Dr. Gilbert's "officiator"—the word servant was abolished as non-republican—announced at nine in the evening that his carriage was at the door.

He donned his hat, buttoned up his outer coat, and was going out, when he saw the door-way blocked by a man in a cloak and a slouch hat. Gilbert recoiled a step, for all was hostile that came in the dark at such a period.

"It is I, Gilbert," said a kindly voice.

"Cagliostro!" exclaimed the doctor.

"Good; there you are forgetting again that I am no longer under that name, but bear that of Baron Zannone. At the same time, Gilbert, for you I am changed in neither name nor heart, and am ever your Joseph Balsamo, I hope."

"Yes; and the proof is that I was going to find you."

"I suspected as much, and that is what has brought me," said the magician. "For you can imagine that in such times I do not go into the country, as Robespierre is doing."

"That is why I feared that I should not find you at home, and I am happy to meet you. But come in, I beg."

"Well, here I am. Say your wish," said Cagliostro, following the master into the most retired room.

"Do you know what is going on?" asked the host, as soon as both were seated.

"You mean what is going to happen; for at present nothing is doing," observed the other.

"No, you are right; but something dreadful is brewing, eh?"

"Dreadful, in sooth; but such is sometimes needful."

"Master, you make me shudder," said Gilbert, "when you utter such sayings with your inexorable coolness."

"I can not help it. I am but the echo of fate."

Gilbert hung his head.

"Do you recall what I told you when I warned you of the fate of Marquis Favras?"

The physician started; strong in facing most men, he felt weak as a child before this mysterious character.

"I told you," went on the enigma, "that if the king had a grain of common sense, which I hoped he had not, he would exercise the wish for self-preservation to flee."

"He did so."

"Yes; but I meant while it was in good time; it was, you know, too late when he went. I added, you may remember, that if he and the queen and the nobles remained, I would bring on the Revolution."

"You are right again, for the Revolution rules," said Gilbert, with a sigh.

"Not completely, but it is getting on. Do you further recall that I showed you an instrument invented by a friend of mine, Doctor Guillotin? Well, that beheading machine, which I exhibited in a drinking-glass to the future queen at Taverney Manor, you will remember, though you were but a boy at the time—no higher than that—yet already courting Nicole—the same Nicole whose husband, Beausire, by the way, is being hung at the present speaking—not before he deserved it! Well, that machine is hard at work."

"Too slowly, since swords and pikes have to be supplementing its blade," said Gilbert.

"Listen," said Cagliostro; "you must grant that we have a most block-headed crew to deal with. We gave the aristocrats, the court, and the monarchs

165

all sorts of warnings without their profiting or being advised by them. We took the Bastile, their persons from Versailles, their palace in Paris; we shut up their king in the temple, and the aristocrats in the other prisons; and all serves for no end. The king, under lock and bolt, rejoices at the Prussians taking his towns, and the lords in the abbey cheer the Germans. They drink wine under the noses of poor people who can not get wholesome water, and eat truffle pies before beggars who can not get bread. On King Wilhelm of Prussia being notified that if he passes Longwy into French territory, as it will be the warrant for the king's death, he replies: 'However imbittered may be the fate of the royal family, our armies must not retrograde. I hope with all my heart to arrive in time to save the King of France, but my duty before all is to save Europe.' And he marches forward to Verdun. It is fairly time to end this nonsense."

"End with whom?" cried Gilbert.

"With the king, the queen, and their following."

"Would you murder a king and a queen?"

"Oh, no; that would be a bad blunder. They must be publicly tried, condemned, and executed, as we have the example set by the execution of Charles I. But, one way or another, doctor, we must get rid of them, and the sooner the better."

"Who has decided this?" protested Gilbert. "Let me hear. Is it the intelligence, the honor, and the conscience of the people of whom you speak? When genius, loyalty, and justice were represented by Mirabeau, Lafayette, and Vergniaud, if you had said 'Louis must die,' in the name of those three I should still have shuddered, but I should doubt. In whose name do you pronounce now? Hissed actors, paltry editors, hot-heads like Marat, who have to be bled to cool them when they shriek for thousands of heads. Leave these failures who think they are wonders because they can undo in a stroke the work which it has taken nature a few score years, for they are villains, master, and you ought not to associate with such burlesques of men."

"My dear Gilbert, you are mistaken again," said the prime mover; "they are not villains; you misuse the word. They are mere instruments."

"Of destruction."

"Ay; but for the benefit of an idea. The enfranchisement of the people, Gilbert; liberty, the Republic—not merely French—God forbid me having so selfish an idea! but universal, the federation of the free world. No, these men have not genius, or honor, or conscience, but something stronger, more inexorable, less resistible—they have instinct."

"Like Attila's."

"You have hit it. Of Attila, who called himself the Scourge of God, and came with the barbaric blood of the north to redeem Roman civilization, corrupted by the feasting, debauched emperors."

"But, in brief, to sum up instead of generalizing, whither will tend a massacre?" asked Gilbert.

"To a plain issue. We will compromise the Assembly and Commune and the people of Paris. We must soak Paris in blood; for you understand that Paris is the brain of France, or of Europe, so that Paris, feeling that there is no forgiveness possible for her, will rise like one man, urge France before her, and hurl the enemy off the sacred soil."

"But you are not a Frenchman; what odds is it to you?" asked Gilbert.

"You were not an American, but you were glad to have the rebel Paul Jones take you to America and aid the rebels to free the Colonies from the British yoke. How can a man of superior mettle and intelligence say to another: 'Do not meddle with us, for you are not French?' Are not the affairs of France those of the world? Is France working solely for herself now, think you? Hark you, Gilbert; I have debated all these points with a mind far stronger than yours—the man or devil named Althotas; and one day he made a calculation of the quantity of blood which must be shed before the sun rises on the free world. His reasonings did not shake my conviction. I marched on, I march on, and on I shall march, overturning all that stands in my path, and saying to myself, in a calm voice, as I look around with a serene look: Woe to the obstacle, for this is the future which is coming! Now you have the pardon of some one to ask? I grant it beforehand. Tell me the name of the man or the woman?"

"I wish to save a woman whom neither of us, master, can allow to die."

"The Countess of Charny?"

"The mother of Sebastian Gilbert."

"You know that it is Danton who, as Minister of Justice, has the prison keys."

"Yes; but I also know that the chief of the Invisibles can say to Danton, 'Open or shut that door.'"

Cagliostro rose, and going over to a writing-desk, wrote a cabalistic sign on a small square of paper. Presenting this to Gilbert, he said:

"Go and find Danton, and ask him anything you like." Gilbert rose.

"What are you going to do when the king's turn comes?"

"I intend to be elected to the convention, so as to vote with all my power against his death."

"Be it so; I can understand that," said the leader. "Act as your conscience dictates, but promise me one thing."

"What is it?"

"There was a time when you would have promised without a condition, Gilbert."

"At that time you would not have told me that a nation could heal itself by murdering, or a people gain by massacre."

"Have it your own way. Only promise me that, when the king shall be executed, you will follow the advice I give you."

"Any advice from the master will be precious," he said, holding out his hand.

"And will be followed?" persisted Cagliostro.

"I swear, if not hurtful to my conscience."

"Gilbert, you are unjust. I have offered you much; have I ever required aught of you?"

"No, master," was Gilbert's reply; "and now, furthermore, you give me a life dearer than mine own."

"Go," said the arch-revolutionist, "and may the genius of France, one of whose noblest sons you are, ever guide you."

The count went out, and Gilbert followed him, stepping into the carriage still waiting, to be driven to the Minister of Justice.

Danton was waiting for one of two things: if he turned to the Commune, he and Marat and Robespierre would rule, and he wanted neither of them. Unfortunately, the Assembly would not have him, and its support to rule alone was the other alternative.

When Gilbert came, he had been wrestling with his wife, who guessed that the massacre was determined upon. He had told her that she talked like a woman in asking him to die rather than let the red tide flow on.

"You say that you will die of the stain, and that my sons will blush for me. No; they will be men some day, and if true Dantons, they will carry their heads high; if weak, let them deny me. If I let them commence the massacre by me, for opposing it, do you know what will become of the revolution between that blood-thirsty maniac, Marat, and that sham utopist, Robespierre? I will stay the bloodshed if I can, and if not, I will take all the guilt on my shoulders. The burden will not prevent me marching to my goal, only I shall be the more terrible."

Gilbert entered.

"Come, Doctor Gilbert, I have a word for you."

Opening a little study door, he led the visitor into it.

"How can I be useful to you?" he asked.

Gilbert took out the paper the Invisible had given him and presented it to Danton.

"Ha! you come on his account, do you? What do you desire?"

"The liberation of a woman prisoned in the abbey."

"The name?"

"The Countess of Charny."

Danton took a sheet of paper and wrote the release.

"There it is," he said; "are there others you would wish to save? Speak; I should like to save some of the unfortunates."

"I have all my desire," said Gilbert, bowing.

"Go, doctor," said the minister; "and when you need anything of me, apply direct. I am happy to do anything for you, man to man. Ah," he muttered at the door, in showing him out, "if I had only your reputation, doctor, as an honorable man!"

Bearer of the precious paper which assured Andrea's life, the father of her son hastened to the abbey. Though nearly midnight, threatening groups still hung round the door. Gilbert passed through the midst of them and knocked at it. The gloomy panel in the low arched way was opened. Gilbert shuddered as he went through—it was to be the way to the tomb.

The order, presented to the warden, stated that instant release was to be given to the person whom Dr. Gilbert should point out. He named the Countess of Charny, and the governor ordered a turnkey to lead Gilbert to the prisoner's cell.

The doctor followed the man up three flights of a spiral staircase, where he entered a cell lighted by a lamp.

Pale as marble, in mourning, a woman sat at a table bearing the lamp, reading a shagreen prayer-book adorned with a silver cross. A brand of fire burned in the fire-place. In spite of the sound of the door opening, she did not lift her eyes; the steps approaching did not move her; she appeared absorbed in her book, but it was absence of mind, for Gilbert stood several minutes without her turning a leaf.

The warder had closed the door, with himself on the outer side.

"My lady the countess," ventured Gilbert, after awhile.

Raising her eyes, Andrea looked without perceiving at first; the veil of her mind was between her and the speaker, but it was gradually withdrawn.

"Ah, and is it you, Doctor Gilbert—what do you want?" she inquired.

"Madame, very ugly rumors are afloat about what is going to happen in the prisons."

"Yes; it is said that the prisoners are to be slaughtered," rejoined Andrea; "but you know, Doctor Gilbert, that I am ready to die."

"I come to take you away madame," he continued, bowing.

"Whither would you take me, doctor?" she asked, in surprise.

"Wherever you like, madame; you are free."

He showed her the release order signed by Danton, which she read; but instead of returning it, she kept it in her hand.

"I might have suspected this," she observed, trying to smile, but she had forgotten the way. "You were sure to try to prevent me dying."

"Madame, there is but one existence which would be dearer to me than my parents', had I ever known my parents—it is yours."

"Yes; and that is why you broke your promise to me."

"I did not, madame, for I sent you the poison."

"By my son?"

"I did not tell you by what hand I should send it."

"In short, you have thought of me, Gilbert. So you entered the lion's den

171

for my sake, and came forthwith the talisman which unseals doors?"

"I told you, madame, that as long as I lived you should not die."

"Nay, Doctor Gilbert, I believe that this time I hold death by the hand," said Andrea, with something more like a smile than her previous attempt.

"Madame, I declare to you that I will stay you from dying, even though I have to employ force."

Without replying, Andrea tore the order into pieces and tossed them into the fire.

"Try it," she said.

Gilbert uttered an outcry.

"Doctor Gilbert," said she, "I have given up the idea of suicide, but not of dying. I long for death."

Gilbert let a groan escape him.

"All that I ask of you is that you will save my body from outrage after death—it has not escaped it in life. Count Charny rests in the family vault at Boursonnes. There I spent the happiest days of my life, and I wish to repose by him."

"Oh, in Heaven's name, I implore you—"

"And I implore you in the name of my sorrow—"

"It is well, lady; you were right in saying that I am bound to obey you in all points. I go, but I am not vanquished."

"Do not forget my last wish."

"If I do not save you in spite of yourself, it shall be accomplished," replied Gilbert.

Saluting her for the last time, he went forth, and the door banged to with that lugubrious sound peculiar to prison doors.

CHAPTER XXIII. THE DEATH OF THE COUNTESS.

In the night, while Gilbert was vainly trying to save Andrea, the Commune, unable to secure Danton's help, formed a committee of vigilance, including Marat, though he was not a member of the Commune. But his name enthroned murder, and showed the frightful development of his power.

The first order of this committee was to have twenty-four prisoners removed from the abbey, and brought before them at the mayor's offices— now the police prefecture building.

It was expected that they would be set upon in the streets, and the butchery there begun would be introduced into the prisons.

Marat's "barkers," as they were called, in vain, however, shouted as the hacks went along:

"Look at the traitors—the accomplices of the Prussians! There they go who are surrendering our towns, slaying our wives and babes, and will do it here if you leave them in the rear when you march to the border."

But, as Danton said, massacres are a scarce bird, and the incitement only brought out more uproar.

Fortune came to the ruffians' assistance.

At a crossing was a stage run up for the voluntary enlistments. The cabs had to stop. A man pushed through the escort and plunged his sword several times inside a carriage, drawing it out dripping with blood. A prisoner had a cane, and trying to parry the steel, he struck one of the guards.

"Why, you brigands," said the struck man, "we are protecting you and you strike us! Lay on, friends!"

Twenty scoundrels, who only waited for the call, sprung out of the throng, armed with knives tied to poles in the way of spears, and stabbed through the carriage windows. The screams arose from inside the conveyances, and the blood trickled out and left a track on the road-way.

Blood calls for blood, and the massacre commenced which was to last four days.

It was regularized by Maillard, who wanted to have every act done in legal style. His registry exists, where his clear, steady handwriting is perfectly calm and legible in the two notes and the signature. "Executed by the judgment of the people," or "Acquitted by the people," and "Maillard."

The latter note appears forty-three times, so that he saved that number.

After the fourth of September he disappeared, swallowed up in the sea of blood.

Meanwhile, he presided over the court. He had set up a table and called for a blank book; he chose a jury, or rather assistant judges, to the number of twelve, who sat six on either side of him.

He called out the prisoner's name from a register; while the turnkeys went for the person, he stated the case, and looked for a decision from his associates as soon as the accused appeared. If condemned, he said: "To Laforce!" which seemed to mean the prison of that name; but the grim pun, understood, was that he was to be handed over to "brute force."

Beyond the outer door the wretch fell under the blows of the butchers.

If the prisoner was absolved, the black phantom rose, laid his hand on the person's head, and said, "Put him out!" and the prisoner was freed.

When Maillard arrived at the Abbey Prison, a man, also in black, who was waiting by the wall, stepped forward to meet him. On the first words exchanged between them, Maillard recognized this man, and bowed his tall figure to him in condescension, if not submission. He brought him into the prison, and when the tribunal was arranged, he said:

"Stand you there, and when the person comes out in whom you are interested, make me a sign."

The man rested his elbow against the wall and stood mute, attentive, and motionless as when outside.

It was Honore Gilbert, who had sworn that he would not let Andrea die, and was still trying to fulfill his oath.

Between four and six in the morning, the judges and butchers took a rest, and at six had breakfast.

At half past the horrid work was resumed.

In that interval such of the prisoners as could see the slaughter out of a window reported by which mode death came swiftest and with the least suffering; they concluded it was by a stab to the heart.

Thereupon, some took turn after turn with a pocket-knife to cheat the slaughterers.

In the midst of this dreadful ante-chamber of death, one woman in deep mourning was kneeling in prayer and smiling.

It was the Countess of Charny.

Two hours yet passed before she was called as "Citizeness Andrea of Taverney, previously known as the Countess of Charny."

At the name, Gilbert felt his legs yield under him and his heart weaken.

A life, more important than his own, was to be debated, tried, and doomed or spared.

"Citizens," said Maillard, "the person about to appear before you is a poor woman who was devoted formerly to the Austrian, but with truly royal ingratitude, she paid her with sorrow; to that friendship she gave all—her property and her husband. You will see her come in, dressed in mourning, which she owes to the prisoner in the temple. Citizens, I ask you for the life of this woman."

The bench of judges nodded; but one said the prisoner ought to appear before them.

"Then, look," said the chief.

The door opening, they saw in the corridor depths a woman clad wholly in black, with her head crowned with a black veil, who walked forward alone without support, with a steady step. She seemed an apparition from another world, at the sight of which even those justices shuddered.

Arriving at the table, she lifted her veil. Never had beauty less disputable but none more pale met the eyes of man; it was a goddess in marble.

All eyes were fixed upon her, while Gilbert panted.

"Citizen"—she addressed Maillard in a voice as sweet as firm—"you are the president?"

"Yes, citizeness," replied the judge, startled at his being questioned.

"I am the Countess of Charny, wife of the count of that house, killed on the infamous tenth of August; an aristocrat and the bosom friend of the queen, I have deserved death, and I come to seek it."

The judges uttered a cry of surprise, and Gilbert turned pale and shrunk as far as he could back into the angle by the door to escape Andrea's gaze.

"Citizens," said Maillard, who saw the doctor's plight, "this creature has gone mad through the death of her husband; let us pity her, and let her senses have a chance to come back. The justice of the people does not fall on the insane."

He rose and was going to lay his hands on Andrea's head as he did when he pronounced those innocent; but she pushed aside his hand.

"I have my full reason," she said; "and if you want to pardon any one, let it be one who craves it and merits it, but not I, who deserve it not and reject it."

Maillard turned to Gilbert and saw that he was wringing his clasped hands.

"This woman is plainly mad," he said; "put her out."

He waved his hand to a member of the court, who shoved the countess toward the door of safety.

"Innocent," he called out; "let her go out."

They who had the weapons ready parted before Andrea, lowered them unto this image of mourning. But, after having gone ten paces, and while Gilbert, clinging to the window bars, saw her going forth, she stopped.

"God save the king!" she cried. "Long live the queen, and shame on the tenth of August!"

Gilbert uttered a shriek and darted out into the yard. For he had seen a sword glitter, and swift as a lightning flash, the blade disappeared in Andrea's bosom. He arrived in time to catch her in his arms, and as she turned on him her dying gaze she recognized him.

"I told you that I would die in spite of you," she muttered. "Love Sebastian for both of us," she added, in a barely intelligible voice, and still more faintly continued: "You will have me laid to rest by him—next my George, my husband, for time everlasting?"

And she expired.

Gilbert raised her up in his arms, while fifty blood-smeared hands menaced him all at once.

But Maillard appeared behind him and said, as he spread his hands over his head:

"Make way for the true citizen Gilbert, carrying out the body of a poor crazed woman slain by mistake."

They stepped aside, and carrying the corpse of Andrea, the man who had first loved her, even to committing crime to triumph over her, passed amid the murderers without one thinking of barring the way, so sovereign was Maillard's words over the multitude.

CHAPTER XXIV. THE ROYAL MARTYR.

Let us return to the somber edifice confining a king become mere man, a queen still a queen, a maid who would be a martyr, and two poor children innocent, from age if not by birth.

The king was in the temple, not the temple tower, but the palace of the Knights Templars, which had been used by Artois as a pleasure resort.

The Assembly had not haggled about his keep, but awarded a handsome sum for the table of one who was a hearty eater, like all the Bourbons. Not only did the judges reprimand him for his untimely gluttony during his trial, but they had a note made of the fact to be on record to our times.

In the temple he had three servants and thirteen attendants connected with the table. Each day's dinner was composed of four entrées—six varieties of roast meat, four fancy dishes, three kinds of stews, three dishes of fruit, and Bordeaux, Madeira, and Malvoisie wine.

He and his son alone drank wine, as the queen and the princesses used water.

On the material side, he had nothing to complain of; but he lacked air, exercise, sunshine, and shady trees.

Habituated by hunting in the royal forests to glade and covert, he had to content himself with a green yard, where a few withered trees scattered prematurely blighted leaves on four parterres of yellowed grass.

Every day at four, the royal family were "walked out" here, as if they were so many head of stall-fed cattle.

This was mean, unkind, ferocious in its cruelty; but less cruel and ferocious than the cells of the pope's dungeons where they had tried to drive Cagliostro to death, or the leads of Venice, or the Spielberg dungeons.

We are not excusing the Commune, and not excusing kings; we are bound to say that the temple was a retaliation, terrible and fatal, but clumsy, for it was making a prosecution a persecution and a criminal a martyr.

What did they look like now—those whom we have seen in their glory?

The king, with his weak eyes, flabby cheeks, hanging lips, and heavy, carefully poised step, seemed a good farmer upset by a great disaster; his melancholy was that of an agriculturist whose barn had been burned by lightning or his fields swept by a cyclone. The queen's attitude was as usual, stiff, proud, and dreadfully irritating. Marie Antoinette had inspired love of grandeur in her time; in her decline, she inspired devotion, but never pity; that springs from sympathy, and she was never one for fellow-feeling.

The guardian angel of the family was Princess Elizabeth, in her white dress, symbol of her purity of body and soul; her fair hair was the handsomer from the disuse of powder. The princess royal, notwithstanding the charm of youth, little interested any one; a thorough Austrian like her mother, her look had already the scorn and arrogance of vultures and royal races. The little dauphin was more winning from his sickly white complexion and golden hair; but his eye was a hard raw blue, with an expression at times older than his age. He understood things too well, caught the idea from a glance of his mother's eye, and showed politic cunning which sometimes wrung tears from those who tormented him.

The Commune were cruel and imprudent; they changed the watchers daily, and sent spies, under the guise of town officers. These went in sworn enemies to the king and came out enemies to the death of Marie Antoinette, but almost all pitying the king, sorrowing for the children, and glorifying the Lady Elizabeth. Indeed, what did they see at the prison? Instead of the wolf, the she-wolf and the whelps—an ordinary middle-class family, with the mother rather the gray mare and spitfire, who would not let any one touch the hem of her dress, but of a brood of tyrants not a trace.

The king had taken up Latin again in order to educate his son, while the queen occupied herself with her daughter. The link of communication between the couple was the valet, Clery, attached to the prince royal, but from the king's own servant, Hue, being dismissed, he waited on both. While hair-dressing for the ladies, he repeated what the king wanted to transmit, quickly and in undertones.

The queen would often interrupt her reading to her daughter by plunging into deep and gloomy musing; the princess would steal away on tiptoe to let her enjoy a new sorrow, which at least had the benefit of tears, and make a hushing sign to her brother. When the tear fell on her ivory hand, beginning to yellow, the poor prisoner would start back from her dream, her momentary freedom in the immense domain of thought and memories, and look round her prison with a lowered head and broken heart.

Weather permitting, the family had a walk in the garden at one o'clock, with a corporal and his squad of the National Guard to watch them. Then the king went up to his rooms on the third story to dine. It was then that Santerre came for his rigorous inspection. The king sometimes spoke with him; the queen never; she had forgotten what she owed to this man on the twentieth of June.

As we have stated, bodily needs were tyrannical in the king, who always indulged in an after-dinner nap; during this, the others remained silent around his easy-chair. Only when he woke was the chat resumed.

When the newsboys called out the news items in the evening, Clery listened, and repeated what he caught to the king.

After supper, the king went into the queen's room to bid her good-night, as well as his sister, by a wave of the hand, and going into his library, read till midnight. He waited before going off to sleep to see the guards changed, to know whether he had a strange face for the night-watcher.

This unchanging life lasted till the king left the small tower—that is, up to September 30th.

It was a dull situation, and the more worthy of pity as it was dignifiedly supported. The most hostile were softened by the sight. They came to watch over the abominable tyrant who had ruined France, massacred Frenchmen, and called the foreigners in; over the queen who had united the lubricities of Messalina to the license of Catherine II.; but they found a plain old fellow whom they could not tell from his valet, who ate and drank heartily and slept soundly, playing piquet or backgammon, teaching Latin and geography to his boy, and putting puzzles to his children out of old newspapers; and a wife, proud and haughty, one must admit, but calm, dignified, resigned, still handsome, teaching her daughter tapestry-work and her son his prayers, speaking gently to the servants and calling them "friends."

The result was that the more the Commune abased the prisoner, and the more he showed that he was like any other man, the more other men took pity on their fellow-man.

Still, all who came into contact with the royal family did not feel the same respect and pity. Hatred and revenge were so deeply rooted in these, that the sight of the regal misery supported with domestic virtues, only brought out rudeness, insults, and actual indignities.

On the king saying that he thought a sentry was tired, the soldier pressed his hat on the more firmly, and said, in the teeth of the monarch:

"My place here is to keep an eye on you and not for you to criticise me. Nobody has the right to meddle with my business, and you least of all."

Once the queen ventured to ask a town officer where he came from.

"I belong to the country," he loftily replied, "at least, as much of it as your foreign friends have not taken possession of."

One day a municipal officer said to Clery, loud enough for the king to overhear: "I would guillotine the lot of them if the regular executioner backed out."

The sentinels decked the walls, where the royals came along to go into the garden, with lines in this style: "The guillotine is a standing institution and is waiting for the tyrant Louis."—"Madame Veto will soon dance on nothing."—"The fat hog must be put on short rations."—"Pull off the red ribbon he wears—it will do to strangle his cubs with."

One drawing represented a man hanging, and was labeled: "Louis taking an air-bath."

The worst tormentors were two lodgers in the temple, Rocher, the sapper, and Simon, the notorious cobbler. The latter, whose harsh treatment of the royal child has made him noted, was insult personified. Every time he saw the prisoners, it was to inflict a fresh outrage.

Rocher was the man whom we saw take up the dauphin when Charny fell, and carry him into the House; yet he, placed by Manuel to prevent harm befalling the captives, resembled those boys who are given a bird to keep—they kill time by plucking out the feathers one by one.

But, however unhappy the prisoners were, they had yet the comfort that they were under the same roof.

The Commune resolved to part the king from his family.

Clery had an inkling of the intention, but he could not get at the exact date until a general searching of the prisoners on the twenty-ninth of September gave him a hint. That night, indeed, they took away the king into rooms in the great tower which were wet with plaster and paint and the smell was unbearable.

But the king lay down to sleep without complaining, while the valet passed the night on a chair.

When he was going out to attend to the prince, whose attendant he strictly was, the guard stopped him, saying:

"You are no longer to have communications with the other prisoners; the king is not to see his children any more."

As they omitted to bring special food for the servant, the king broke his bread with him, weeping while the man sobbed.

When the workmen came to finish the rooms, the town officer who superintended them came up to the king with some pity, and said:

"Citizen, I have seen your family at breakfast, and I undertake to say that all were in health."

The king's heart ached at this kind feeling.

He thanked the man, and begged him to transmit the report of his health to his dear ones. He asked for some books, and as the man could not read, he accompanied Clery down into the other rooms to let him select the reading matter. Clery was only too glad, as this gave an opportunity of seeing the queen. He could not say more than a few words, on account of the soldiers being present.

The queen could not hold out any longer, and she besought to let them all have a meal in company.

The municipal officers weakened, and allowed this until further orders. One of them wept, and Simon said:

"Hang me if these confounded women will not get the water-works running in my eyes. But," he added, addressing the queen, "you did not do any weeping when you shot down the people on the tenth of August."

"Ah!" said the queen; "the people have been much misled about our feelings toward them. If you knew us better, you would be sorry, like this gentleman."

So the dinner was served in the old place; it was a feast, for they gained so much in one day, they thought. They gained everything, for nothing more was heard of the Commune's new regulation; the king continued to see his family daily, and to take his meals with them.

One of these days, when he went in, he found the queen sweeping up the dauphin's room, who was unwell. He stopped on the sill, let his head sink on his breast, and sighed:

"Ah, my lady, this is sorry work for a Queen of France, and if they could see from Vienna what you are doing here! Who would have thought that, in uniting you to my fate, I should ever bring you so low?"

"Do you reckon it as nothing," replied Marie Antoinette, "this glory of being the wife of the best and most persecuted of men?"

This was spoken without an idea there were hearers; but all such sayings were picked up and diffused to embroider with gold the dark legend of the martyr king.

CHAPTER XXV. MASTER GAMAIN TURNS UP.

One morning, while these events were occurring at the temple, a man wearing a red shirt and cap to match, leaning on a crutch to help him to hobble along, called on the Home Secretary, Roland. The minister was most accessible; but even a republican official was forced to have ushers in his antechamber, as went on in monarchical governments.

"What do you want?" challenged the servant of the man on the crutch.

"I want to speak with the Citizen Minister," replied the cripple.

Since a fortnight, the titles of citizen and citizeness had officially replaced all others.

"You will have to show a letter of audience," replied the domestic.

"Halloo! I thought that was all very fine fun in the days when the tyrant ruled, but folks ought to be equals under the Republic, or at least not so aristocratic."

This remark set the servant thinking.

"I can tell you that it is no joke," continued the man in red, "to drag all the way from Versailles to do the Secretary of State a service and not to get a squint of him."

"Oh, you come to do Citizen Roland a service, do you?"

"To show up a conspiracy."

"Pooh! we are up to our ears in conspiracies. If that is all you came from Versailles for, I suggest you get back."

"I don't mind; but your minister will be deuced sorry for not seeing me."

"It is the rule. Write to him and get a letter of audience; then you will get on swimmingly."

"Hang me if it is not harder to get a word in to Minister Roland than to his majesty Louis XVI. that was."

"What do you know about that?"

"Lord help your ignorance, young man; there was a time when I saw the king whenever I pleased; my name would tell you that."

"What is your name? Are you King Frederick William or the Emperor Francis?"

"No; I am not a tyrant or a slave-driver—no aristo—but just Nicholas Claude Gamain, master of the masters of my trade of locksmithery. Did you never hear of Master Gamain who taught the craft to old Capet?"

The footman looked questioningly at his fellows, who nodded.

"Then it is another pair of shoes. Write your name on a sheet of paper, and I will send it in to the Home Secretary."

"Write? It is all very easy to say write, but I was no dabster at the pen before these villains tried to poison me; and it is far worse now. Just look how they doubled me up with arsenic."

He showed his twisted legs, deviated spine, and hand curled up like a claw.

"What! did they serve you out thus, poor old chap?"

"They did. And that is what I have come to show the Citizen Minister, along with other matters. As I hear they are getting up the indictment against old Capet, what I have to tell must not be lost for the nation."

Five minutes afterward, the locksmith was shown into the official's presence.

The master locksmith had never, at the height of his fortune and in the best of health, worn a captivating appearance; but the malady to which he was a prey, articular rheumatism in plain, while twisting his limbs and disfiguring his features, had not added to his embellishments. The outcome was that never had an honest man faced a more ruffianly looking rogue than Roland when left alone with Gamain.

The minister's first feeling was of repugnance; but seeing how he trembled from head to foot, pity for a fellow-man, always supposing that a wretch like Gamain is a fellow to a Roland, led him to use as his first words:

"Take a seat, citizen; you seem in pain."

"I should rather think I am in pain," replied Gamain, dropping on a chair; "and I have been so ever since the Austrian poisoned me."

At these words a profound expression of disgust passed over the hearer's countenance, while he exchanged a glance with his wife, half hidden in the window recess.

"And you came to denounce this poisoning?"

"That and other things."

"Do you bring proof of your accusations?"

"For that matter, you have only to come with me to the Tuileries and I will give you piles of it. I will show you the secret hole in the wall where the brigand hid his hoard. I ought to have guessed that the wine was poisoned that the Austrian sneaked out to offer me, a-saying, with her wheedling voice: 'Here you are, Gamain! drink this glass of wine; it will do you good now the work is done.'"

"Poisoned?"

"Yes; everybody knows," continued Gamain, with sullen hate, "that those who help kings to conceal treasures never make old bones."

"There is something at the bottom of this," said Mme. Roland, coming forward at his glance; "this was the smith who was the king's tutor. Ask him about the hole in the wall."

"The press?" said Gamain, who had overheard. "Why, I am here to lay that open. It is an iron safe, with a lock-bolt working both ways, in which

Citizen Capet hid his private papers and savings."

"How did you come to know about it?"

"Did he not send for me to show him how to finish the lock, one he made himself, and of course would not work smoothly?"

"But this press would be smashed and rifled in the capture of the Tuileries."

"There is no danger of that. I defy anybody in the world to get the idea of it, barring him and me."

"Are you sure?"

"Sure and certain. It is just the same as when he left the Tuileries."

"What do you say to all this, Madeleine?" asked Roland of his wife, when they had listened to Gamain's story, told in his prolix style.

"I say the revelation is of the utmost importance, and no time must be lost in verifying it."

The secretary rang for his carriage, whereupon Gamain stood up sulkily.

"I see you have had enough of me," he grumbled.

"Why, no; I only ring for my carriage."

"What! do ministers have carriages under the Republic?"

"They have to do so, to save time, my friend. I call the carriage so that we shall be quickly at the Tuileries. But what about the key to the safe?—it is not likely Louis XVI. left it in the key-hole."

"Why, certainly not, for our fat Capet is not such a fool as he looks. Here is a duplicate," he continued, drawing a new key from his pocket; "I made it from memory. I tell you I am the master of my craft. I studied the lock, fancying some day—"

"This is an awful scoundrel," said Roland to his wife.

"Yes; but we have no right to reject any information coming to us in the

187

present state of affairs in order to arrive at a knowledge of the truth. Am I to go with you?" asked the lady.

"Certainly, as there are papers in the case. Are you not the most honest man I know?"

Gamain followed them to the door, mumbling:

"I always said that I would pay old Capet out for what he did to me. What Louis XVI. did was kindness."

CHAPTER XXVI. THE TRIAL OF THE KING.

On the seventh of November the Girondists began the indictment against the king, assisted by the fatal deposit of papers in the iron safe, although those were missing which were confided to Mme. Campan. After Gamain's opening the press, which was to have so severe an effect on the prisoners in the temple, Roland had taken them all to his office, where he read them and docketed them, though he vainly searched for the evidence of Danton's oft-cited venality. Besides, Danton had resigned as Minister of Justice.

This great trial was to crown the victory of Valmy, which had made the defeated King of Prussia almost as angry as the news of the proclamation of the Republic in Paris.

This trial was another step toward the goal to which men blundered like the blind, always excepting the Invisibles; they saw things in the mass, but not in detail. Alone on the horizon stood the red guillotine, with the king at the foot of the scaffold on which it rose.

In a materialistic era, when such a man as Danton was the head of the indulgent party, it was difficult for the wish not to be outrun by the deed; yet only a few of the Convention comprehended that royalty should be extirpated, and not the royal person slain.

Royalty was a somber abstraction, a menacing mystery of which men were weary, a whited sepulcher, fair without, but full of rottenness.

But the king was a different matter; a man who was far from interesting in his prosperity, but purified by misfortune and made great by captivity. Even on the queen the magic of adversity was such that she had learned, not to love—for her broken heart was a shattered vase from which the precious ointment had leaked out—but to venerate and adore, in the religious sense of the word, this prince, though a man whose bodily appetite and vulgar instincts had so often caused her to blush.

Royalty smitten with death, but the king kept in perpetual imprisonment, was a conception so grand and mighty that but few entertained it.

"The king must stand trial," said the ex-priest Gregoire to the Convention; "but he has done so much to earn scorn that we have no room for hatred."

And Tom Paine wrote:

"I entreat you to go on with the trial, not so much of this king as the whole band of them; the case of this individual whom you have in your power will put you on the track of all. Louis XVI. is useful as showing the necessity of revolutions."

So great minds like Paine and great hearts like Gregoire were in tune on this point. The kings were to be tried, and Louis might even be allowed to turn state's evidence.

This has never been done, but it is good yet to do. Suppose the charge against the Empress Catherine, Pasiphæ of the north; who will say there would not come out instruction to the world from such a revelation?

To the great disappointment of the Rolands, we repeat, the papers in the iron safe did not compromise Dumouriez and Danton, while they earned Gamain a pension, little alleviating the pangs of his ailment, which made him a thousand times regret the guillotine to which he consigned his master. But they injured the king and the priests, showing up the narrow mind, sharp and ungrateful, of Louis, who only hated those who wanted to save him—Necker, Lafayette, and Mirabeau. There was nothing detrimental to the Girondists.

Who was to read the dread indictment? Who was to be the sword-bearer and float over the court like the destroying angel? St. Just, the pet of Robespierre, a pale young man with womanly lips, who uttered the atrocious words. The point was that the king must be killed. The speech made a terrible impression; not one of the judges but felt the repeated word enter his soul like steel. Robespierre was appalled to see his disciple plant the red flag of revolution so far ahead of the most advanced outposts of republicanism.

As time progressed, the watch over the prisoners was closer, and Clery could learn nothing; but he picked up a newspaper stating that Louis would be brought before the bar of the House on the eleventh of December.

Indeed, at five that morning the reveille was beaten all over Paris. The temple gates were opened to bring in cannon; but no one would tell the captives the meaning of the unusual stir.

Breakfast was the last meal they partook of in company; when they parted, the prince was left playing a numerical game with his father, who kept the truth from him.

"Curse sixteen," said the boy, on losing three times running; "I believe you are bad luck!"

The king was struck by the figure.

At eleven the dauphin was removed and the king left in silence, as the officials did not intrude, for fear he would question them. At one o'clock Santerre arrived with officers, and a registrar who read the decree calling "the prisoner Louis Capet" before the House.

The king interrupted to say that Capet was not his name, but that of an ancestor. He stopped the reading on the grounds that he had read it in the papers.

As it was raining, they had a carriage in which to carry him.

On alighting, Santerre laid his hand on his shoulder and led him to the same spot at the bar, by the same chair, where he had taken the oath to the Constitution.

All the members save one had kept their seats as he entered; this one saluted him. The astonished king recognized Gilbert. He wished him good-day.

"Are you acquainted with Doctor Gilbert?" asked Santerre.

"He was my physician once, so I hope no ill feeling will be harbored because he was polite to me."

The examination began. Unfortunately, the glamour of misfortune vanished before duplicity; not only did the king answer the questions put to him, but he did so badly, stammering, hesitating, trying to evade direct issues, chaffering for his life like a pettifogger arguing a party-fence case in a county court.

The king did not appear at his best in broad day.

The examination lasted five hours. Though he refused refreshment offered, he asked a grenadier for a piece of the bread he saw him eating.

On crossing the yard to step into the carriage, the mob sung with marked emphasis the line of the "Marseillaise" about "the impure blood should fertilize our furrows."

This made him lose color.

The return was miserable. In the public hack, swaying on the black, pestiferous, vile pavement, while the mob surged up to the windows to see him, he blinked his eyes at the daylight; his beard was long, and his thin hair of a dirty yellow hue; his thin cheeks fell in folds on his wrinkled neck; clad in a gray suit, with a dark-brown overcoat, he mumbled with the Bourbon's automatic memory: "This is such and such a street."

On remarking that Orleans Street had been changed to Egalite, on account of the duke having dropped his titles, though that did not save him from the guillotine, he fell into silence, and so returned into prison.

He was not allowed to see his family, and had to go to bed without the meal with them.

"Ah, Clery!" he said to his man, as he undressed him, "I little dreamed what questions they were going to put to me."

Indeed, almost all the inquiry was based on the contents of the iron safe, which he did not suspect was discovered, from having no idea that Gamain had betrayed him.

Nevertheless, he soon sunk to sleep with that tranquillity of which he had given so many proofs, and which might be taken for lethargy.

But the other prisoners did not bear the separation and the secrecy so tamely.

In the morning the queen asked to see her husband, but the only arrangement offered was that the king might see his children on condition that they should not see their mother or aunt any more. The king refused this plan.

Consequently, the queen had her son's bed put in her rooms, and she did not quit him till removed for trial by the Revolutionary Tribunal, as her husband was by the Convention.

Clery, however, worked communications with a servant of the princesses named Turgy. They exchanged a few words, and passed notes scratched with pins on scraps of paper, on the ladies' side; the king could write properly, as he had writing materials supplied since his trial commenced.

By means of a string, collected from the pieces around the packets of candles, Clery lowered pens, ink, and paper to Princess Elizabeth, whose window was below that of the valet's room.

Hence the family had news of one another daily.

On the other hand, the king's position was morally much worse since he had appeared before the Convention.

It had been surmised that he would either refuse to answer any interrogation, like Charles I., whose history he knew so well; or else that he would answer proudly and loftily in the name of royalty, not like an accused criminal, but a knight accepting the gage of battle.

Unfortunately, Louis was not regal enough to do either act. He so entangled himself that he had to ask for counsel. The one he named fearing to accept the task, it fell to Malesherbes, who had been in the Turgot Ministry, a commonplace man in whom little did any suspect contempt for death. (On the day of his execution, for he was beheaded, he wound up his watch as usual.) Throughout the trial he styled the king "Sire."

Attacked by a flow of blood to the head, the king asked for Dr. Gilbert to be allowed to attend him, but the application was refused, and he was brutally told that if he drank cold water he would not have such a fullness of blood. As he was not allowed a knife to carve his food, unless a servant did it before the guards, so he was not let shave but in the presence of four municipal officers.

On the evening of the twenty-fifth he wrote his will, in which he said that he did not blame himself for any of the crimes of which he was accused. He did not say that they were false. This evasive response was worthy the pupil of the Duke of Vauguyon.

In any case, the twenty-sixth found him ready for any fate, death included.

His counsel read the defense, which was a purely legal document. It seems to us that if we had been charged with it, we should not have spoken for the law, but let St. Louis and Henry IV. defend their descendants from the crimes of their intermediate successors.

The more unjust the accusation, the more eloquent should have been the rejoinder.

Hence the Convention asked, in astonishment:

"Have you nothing more to say in your defense?"

He had nothing to say, and went back to the temple. When his defender called in the evening, he told him of a number of gentlemen who were pledged to prevent the execution.

"If you do not know them personally," said the king to Lamoignon Malesherbes, "try to come in touch with them and tell them that I will never forgive myself for blood shed on my behalf. I would not have it spilled to save my throne and life, when that was possible; all the more reason for me not allowing it now."

The voting on the 16th of January, 1793, was on three points:

Is Louis guilty? Shall there be an appeal from the Convention to the people? State the penalty.

To the first question was the answer of 683 voices, "Yes."

To the appeal question, 281 ayes and 423 noes.

The third decision of the penalty was subdivided into death, imprisonment, banishment, or death, with the people allowed to reduce it to imprisonment.

All tokens of approval or displeasure were prohibited, but when a member said anything but death, murmurs arose.

Once there were groans and hisses when a member spoke for death— when Philippe Egalite cast his vote for the execution of his kinsman.

The majority for death was seven, and Vergniaud uttered the sentence with deep emotion.

It was three on the morning of the twentieth, Sunday.

The illustrious culprit was up when Malesherbes bore him the news.

"I was sure of it," he said, shaking hands with his defender. "For two days I have been trying to find if I have merited my subjects' reproach for what I have done in the course of my reign. I swear to you in all sincerity, as a man about to appear before his Maker, that I have always wished the happiness of my people, and have not framed a wish contrary to it."

The death-warrant was officially read to him, and he was allowed to choose his own confessor.

The name of one had been already written down by Princess Elizabeth, whose confessor this Abbe Edgeworth was.

CHAPTER XXVII. THE PARALLEL TO CHARLES I.

This worthy priest, of English origin, had escaped the September massacres and was hiding out at Choisy, under the name of Essex, as the Princess Elizabeth knew, and where to find him.

He came to the call, though he believed that he would be killed within an hour of the dreadful scene.

He was not to quit the prisoner till he quitted the world.

The king was allowed to take farewell of his family in the dining-room, where the glass door allowed the guards still to keep him in sight. They knew the trial had taken place, but not the particulars, with which he supplied them. He dwelt particularly on the fact that Petion had not pressed for the death penalty, and that Gilbert had voted to spare his life.

Heaven owed the poor prisoner some comfort, and it came in the love of the queen.

As has been seen in our story, the queen easily let the picturesque side of life attract her. She had that vivid imagination which makes women imprudent even more than disposed; she had been imprudent all her life in her friendship and in her loving.

Her captivity saved her in a moral point of view; she returned to the pure and holy domestic virtues from which youthful passions had led her; and as she could do nothing without extravagance, she fell to loving passionately, in his distress, this royal consort whose vulgar traits were all she could see in the days of felicity. In their first disasters she saw a dullard, almost cowardly, without impulse or resolution; at the temple she began to see that the wife had not only misjudged the husband, but the queen the monarch. She beheld one calm and patient, meek but firm under outrages; all the worldly dryness in her was melted, and turned to the profit of better sentiments.

The same as she had scorned too deeply, she loved too fondly.

"Alas!" the king said to his confessor, "to think that I love so dearly and am loved so much."

In their last interview, the queen seemed to yield to a feeling akin to remorse. When she found that she could not be alone with her lord, she drew him into a window recess, where she would have fallen on her knees at his feet; but he understood that she wanted to ask his forgiveness, so he stayed her and drew his will from his pocket to show her the lines:

"I pray my wife to forgive all the woes I have led her to suffer and the sorrows caused her in the course of our union, as she may be sure that I cherish no ill feeling toward her, if she should think that she had reason to blame herself in any way."

Marie kissed his hands, for while there was full pardon, there was great delicacy, too, in the rest of the phrase.

So this royal Magdalen might die tranquil, late as came her love for her husband, it won her divine and human mercy, and her pardon was bestowed on earth, not in a mysterious whisper as an indulgence, of which the king felt ashamed, but openly and publicly.

Who would reproach her who went toward posterity with the double crown of the martyr and her husband's forgiveness?

The poignant farewell lasted nearly two hours before the condemned went out to his priest.

As day began to break, the drums were beaten throughout the town; the bustle and the sound penetrated the old tower and chilled the blood of the priest and Clery.

At nine o'clock the noise increased and the doors were loudly flung open. Santerre came in, followed by town officers and soldiers, who formed a double row.

The king received the priest's blessing and a prayer for support, and called for his hat, as all the others had kept their hats on. Seeing that Clery had his overcoat ready for fear he would be cold, and the shiver would be taken for that of fright, he said:

"No; nothing but my hat."

He took advantage of the act to shake his hand for the last time.

"Let us go, gentlemen," he said, with the tone of command so rarely used by him.

In crossing the first yard, he turned two or three times to wave a farewell to his dear ones.

With the priest he stepped into a hack, and the procession started, leaving the queen no hope save for a rescue on the road. That of a respite had already vanished.

She fell into a chair, sobbing: "To think of his going without saying good-bye!"

The streets were foggy and deserted, as all citizens were forbidden to be about unless belonging to the armed militia, and there were no faces up at the windows.

All the prisoner saw was a forest of pikes and bayonets, with a large drum corps before the party and cavalry around.

The clamor prevented the king talking with the confessor, who read his prayer-book.

At St. Denis Gate the king lifted his head, for the uproar was marked by a change in the shouts. A dozen young men, sword in hand, rushed through the retinue and shouted:

"Rescue! This way, those who would save the king!"

One Baron de Batz, an adventurer, had engaged three thousand bravoes to make this attempt, but only a handful responded when he sounded the signal-cry. This forlorn hope of royalty, meeting no reply, retreated and slipped away in the confusion.

The incident was of such slight importance that the carriage did not stop; it was at its journey's end when it did.

One of the three brothers Sanson, the Paris executioners, came to open the door.

Laying his hand on the abbe's knee, the king said, in the tone of a master:

"Gentlemen, I recommend this gentleman to you. Take care of him after my death, for he has done nobody harm."

He threw off his coat, not to be touched by the headsman. One had a rope to bind his hands, but he said he would not submit to it. A hand-to-hand fight would rob the victim of all the merit of six months' calmness, courage, and resignation, so the confessor advised him to yield, particularly as one of the Sansons, moved with pity, offered to substitute a handkerchief.

He held out his hands resignedly, saying:

"Do as you like. I shall drain the chalice to the dregs."

The scaffold steps were high and slippery, and he had the priest's arm for support, but on the top step he escaped, so to say, from the spiritual guide, and went to the further end of the platform.

He was flushed in the face, and had never appeared more hale or animated.

The drums began to beat, but he imposed silence by a look as, with a lusty voice, he said:

"I die innocent of all the crimes imputed to me. I forgive the authors of my death, and I pray God that this blood shall not fall on France."

"Strike up, drums!" roared a voice long believed to be Santerre's, but was that of Beaufranchet, Count Oyat, illegitimate son of Louis XV., and a courtesan, the prisoner's natural uncle.

The drums beat, and the king stamped his foot in vain.

"Do your duty!" yelled the pikemen to the executioners, who threw themselves on the king.

He returned with slow steps under the knife, of which he had designed the proper shape only a year ago.

He glanced at the priest who was praying at a corner of the scaffold.

Behind the two upright beams a scuffle went on. The tilting flap fell into place, and the prisoner's head appeared in the ominous gap. A flash, a dull, chopping sound was heard, and a large jet of blood spouted forth.

Then, one of the death's-men taking up the head, sprinkled the bystanders with the dripping fluid. At this sight the pikemen whooped and rushed to dye their weapons in the blood, which they ran to show the town, with shouts of "Long live the Republic!"

For the first time this cry found no echo, though it had oft thrilled hearers with joy. The Republic had a stain on the brow which nothing ever could efface. As a great diplomatist said, it had committed worse than a crime—a blunder.

Thus died, on the 21st of January, 1793, King Louis XVI. He was aged thirty-nine years. He had reigned eighteen, and was over five months a prisoner. His last wish was not accomplished, for his blood not only fell on France, but over the whole of Europe.

CHAPTER XXVIII. CAGLIOSTRO'S ADVICE.

On the evening of this awful day, while the pike-bearers were scouring Paris through streets illuminated but deserted, to exhibit rags dyed in blood, with shouts of "The tyrant is dead! behold his blood!" two men whose dress was different, sat in silence in a room in a house in St. Honore Street.

Dressed in black, one was sitting at a table, with his head resting on his hand, plunged into deep reverie, if not grief. The other, wearing a countryman's dress, strode up and down, with wrinkled forehead, gloomy eye, and folded arms. Every time his crossing line brought him by the table, he cast a glance on the thinker.

At last the countryman stopped and said, as he fixed his eye on the other:

"Come, now, Citizen Gilbert, am I a brigand because I voted for the king's death?"

The man in black raised his head, shook his melancholy brow, and said, holding out his hand to his companion:

"No, Billet, you are no more a brigand for that than I am an aristocrat for voting the other way. You voted according to your conscience, and I to mine. It is a terrible thing to take away from man that which you can not restore."

"So it is your opinion that despotism is inviolable," returned Billet, "liberty is revolt, and there is no justice on earth except such as kings, that is, tyrants, dispense? Then what remains for the people, the right to serve and obey? Do you, Gilbert, the pupil of Rousseau, say that?"

"No, Billet, for that would be an impiety against the people."

"Come," said the farmer, "I am going to talk to you with the roughness of my plain good sense, to which I do not mind your answering with all the sharpness of your fine wit. Do you admit that a nation, believing itself oppressed, should have the right to disestablish its church, lower or even demolish the throne, fight and make itself free?"

"Not a doubt of it."

"Then it has the right to gather in the spoils of the victory?"

"Yes, Billet; but not to compass such things with murder and violence. Remember that it is written, 'Thou shalt not kill thy neighbor.'"

"But the king was no neighbor of mine," returned Billet; "he was my enemy. I remember what my poor mother read me in the Bible of what Samuel said to the Israelites who asked him to appoint a king."

"So do I, Billet; and Samuel anointed Saul—he did not kill him.

"Oh, I know that if I get to arguing with you in book learning, I shall lose. So I simply ask you, were we right to take the Bastile?"

"Yes."

"When the king took away our right to hold a meeting, were we right to meet in another place?"

"You were."

"Had we the right, when the king gathered foreign troops at Versailles to feast them and overawe us, to take him away from among them and lodge him in Paris?"

"Yes."

"To bring him back when he tried to run away from the country?"

"Yes."

"Then we had a right to shut him up where he was so little out of mischief that he continued to correspond with the invader. Ought we not have brought him before the court for trial, to doom him, and—"

"Ay, to banish, to perpetually imprison, all except death, because, guilty in the result, he was not so in the intention. You judge him from the people's standing, Billet; but he acted like the son of kings. Was he a tyrant, as you call him? No. An oppressor of the people? No. An accomplice of aristocrats and an enemy of freedom? No."

"Then you judge him as royalty would?"

"No; for then he would have been acquitted."

"But you did so by voting for his life."

"No; with life imprisonment. Granting he was not your neighbor, but your enemy, he was a vanquished one, and ought not to have been slain in cold blood. That is not execution, but immolation. You have conferred on royalty something like martyrdom, and made justice seem vengeance. Take care! In doing too much, you have not done enough. Charles of England was executed, but his son reigned. But James II. was banished, and his sons died in exile. Human nature is humane, and you have alienated from the Republic for fifty or a hundred years the immense proportion of the population judging revolutions by their feelings. Believe me, my friend, Republicans ought most to bewail the death of Louis, for the blood will fall on them, and cost the Republic its life."

"There is some truth in what you say, Gilbert," said a voice at the door.

"Cagliostro!" exclaimed both debaters, turning with the same impulse.

"Yes; but there is also truth in what Billet said."

"That is the trouble in it," sighed Gilbert; "the cause we plead has two faces, and each, as he looks upon it, can say he is right."

"But he ought also to admit that he may be wrong."

"What is your opinion, master?" asked the doctor.

"Yes, your opinion?" said Billet.

"You have been trying the accused over again, but you should test the sentence. Had you doomed the king, you would have been right. You doomed the man, and you were wrong."

"I don't understand," said Billet.

"You ought to have slain the king amid his guards and courtiers, while unknown to the people—when he was to them a tyrant. But, after having let him live and dwell under the eyes of the private soldier, the petty civil servant, the workman, as a man, this sham abasement elevated him, and he ought to have been banished or locked up, as happens to any man."

"I did not understand you," said Billet to the doctor, "but I do the Citizen Cagliostro."

"Just think of their five months' captivity molding this lump—who was born to be a parish beadle—into a statue of courage, patience, and resignation, on a pedestal of sorrow; you sanctified him so that his wife adored him. Who would have dreamed, my dear Gilbert," said the magician, bursting into laughter, "that Marie Antoinette would ever have loved her mate?"

"Oh, if I had only guessed this," muttered Billet, "I would have slain him before! I could have done it easily."

These words were spoken with such intense patriotism that Gilbert pardoned them, while Cagliostro admired.

"But you did not do it," said the latter. "You voted for death; and you, Gilbert, for life. Now, let me give you a last piece of advice. You, Gilbert, strove to be a member of the convention to accomplish a duty; you, Billet, to fulfill vengeance; both are realized. You have nothing more to do here. Be gone."

The two stared at him.

"To-morrow, your indulgence will be regarded as a crime, and on the next day your severity as bad. Believe me, in the mortal strife preparing between hatred, fear, revenge, fanaticism, few will remain unspotted; some will be fouled with mud, some with blood. Go, my friends, go!"

"But France?" said the doctor.

"Yes, France?" echoed Billet.

"Materially," said Cagliostro, "France is saved; the external enemy is baffled, the home one dead. The Revolution holds the ax in one hand and the tri-colored flag in the other. Go in tranquillity, for before she lays them down, the aristocracy will be beheaded, and Europe conquered. Go, my friends, go to your second country, America!"

"Will you go with me, Billet?" asked the doctor.

"Will you forgive me?" asked Billet.

The two clasped hands.

"You must go at once. The ship 'Franklin' is ready to sail."

"But my son?"

Cagliostro had opened the door.

"Come in, Sebastian," he said; "your father calls you."

The young man rushed into his father's arms, while Billet sighed.

"My carriage is at the door," said Cagliostro. Then, in a whisper to the doctor while Billet was asking news of the youth, he said, emphatically:

"Take him away; he must not know how he lost his mother. He might thirst for revenge."

Gilbert nodded and opened a money drawer.

"Fill your pockets," he said to Billet.

"Will there be enough in a strange country?" he asked.

"Bless you! with land at five dollars an acre, cleared, we can buy a county. But what are you looking round for?"

"For what would be no use to me, who can not write."

"I see; you want to send good-bye to Pitou. Let me."

"What have you written?"

"MY DEAR PITOU,—We are leaving France—Billet, Sebastian, and I—

205

and send you our united love. We think that as you are manager of Billet's farm, you do not need anything. One of these days we may write for you to come over and join us.

"Your friend,

"GILBERT."

"Is that all?" asked the farmer.

"There is a postscript," said the writer, looking the farmer in the face as he said:

"Billet hopes you will take the best of care of Catherine."

Billet uttered a cry of gratitude and shook Gilbert's hand again.

Ten minutes afterward, the post-chaise carried far from Paris Gilbert and his friend and the son of Andrea of Charny.

CHAPTER XXIX. THE CROWN OF ANGE'S LOVE.

A little over a year after the execution of the king and the departure of Gilbert, his son, and Billet, on a fine, cold morning of the hard winter of 1794, three or four hundred persons—that is, a sixth of the population of Villers Cotterets—waited on the square before the manor-house and in the mayor's yard for the coming out of two married folks whom Mayor Longpre was uniting in the holy bonds. These were Ange Pitou and Catherine Billet.

Alas! it had taken many grave events to bring the flame of Viscount Charny, the mother of little Isidore, to become Mistress Pitou.

Everybody was chattering over these events; but in whatever manner they related and discussed them, there was always something to the greater glory of the devotion of Ange Pitou and the good behavior of Billet's daughter.

Only, the more interesting the couple were, the more they were pitied.

Perhaps they were happier than any in the crowd; but human nature is inclined that way—it must pity or applaud!

On this occasion it was in the compassionate vein.

Indeed, what Cagliostro had foreseen, had come on rapidly, leaving a long track of blood after it.

On the 1st of February, 1793, the issue of more paper money was agreed. In March, the fugitive nobles were perpetually banished and their property confiscated. In November, a new kind of religion was proposed instead of the established church.

The result of the confiscation decree was, that Billet and Gilbert being considered fugitives, their lands were seized for the public good. The same fate befell the estates of the Charnys, the count having been killed and the countess murdered in prison.

The consequence to Catherine was that she was turned out of Billet's farm, which was national property. Pitou wanted to protest, but Pitou was a moderate and a "suspect," and wise souls advised him not to oppose the orders of the nation in will or deed.

So Catherine and Pitou had gone over to Haramont.

She had thought of taking refuge in Daddy Clovis's lodge, but he appeared at the door to lay his finger on his lips and shake his head in token of impossibility; the place was already occupied.

The law on the banishment of refractory priests was still in force, and it is easy to understand that Father Fortier had banished himself, as he would not take the oath. But he had not felt like passing the frontier, and his exile was limited to his leaving his house in charge of his sister, to see the furniture was not stolen, and asking Clovis for shelter, which was granted.

This retreat was only a cave, and it would with difficulty hold, in addition to the corpulent priest, Catherine, little Isidore, and Pitou.

Besides, we recall the refusal of the priest to bury Mrs. Billet. Catherine was not good Christian enough to overlook the unkindness, and had she been so, the Abbe Fortier was too good a Catholic to forgive her.

So they had to give up the idea of staying with old Clovis.

This choice lay between Aunt Angelique's house and Pitou's lodgings at Haramont.

They dared not think of the former. As the revolution had followed its course, Angelique had become more and more diabolic, which seems incredible, and thinner, which seems impossible.

This change in her temper and her physique arose from the fact that the churches were closed at Villers as elsewhere, awaiting the invention of a reasonable and civic cult, according to the Board of Public Instruction. The churches being shut, Aunt Angelique's principal revenue, from letting seats, fell into disuse.

It was the drying up of her income which made her Tartar—we beg pardon, tarter and bonier than ever.

Let us add that she had so often heard the story of Pitou and Billet capturing the Bastile, and had so often seen them start off for Paris whenever any great event was to take place, that she did not in the least doubt that the French Revolution was led by Ange Pitou and Farmer Billet, with Citizens Danton, Marat, Robespierre & Co., playing the secondary parts.

The priest's sister fostered her in these somewhat erroneous opinions, to which the regicidal vote of Billet had given the seal on heated fanaticism.

Pitou ought not to think of placing the regicide's daughter under Angelique's roof.

As for the petty accommodation at Haramont, how could he think of installing two—there were three—souls in two rooms; while if they were comfortable, it would set evil tongues wagging?

It was more out of the question than Clovis's hut.

So Pitou made up his mind to beg shelter for himself of Desire Maniquet. That worthy son of Haramont gave the hospitality which Pitou paid for in kind; but all this did not provide Catherine with a fixed habitation.

Pitou showed her all the attentions of a loving friend and the affection of a brother; but poor Catherine was well aware that he did not love her like friend or brother.

Little Isidore had something of the same idea; for the poor child, having never known the Viscount of Charny, loved him more perhaps, for Pitou was not merely the sweetheart of Catherine, but his slave.

A skillful strategist must have understood that the way to win Catherine's heart was through the help of the little one.

But we hasten to say that no such calculation tarnished the purity of Pitou's sentiments. He was just the simple fellow we met him at the first, unless, on becoming a man, he became simpler than ever.

All his good gifts touched Catherine. She saw that Pitou adored her ardently, to the point of fanaticism, and she caught herself wishing that she could repay so great a love and utter devotion with something better than friendship.

Gradually, by dint of dwelling on her isolation from all the world, Pitou excepted, and on her boy being left alone if she were to die, Pitou again excepted, she came to giving Pitou the only reward in her power—her hand.

Alas, her first love, that perfumed flower of youth, was in heaven!

For six months Catherine had been nourishing this conclusion without Pitou suspecting that the wind was blowing up in his favor, though her welcoming was a shade warmer and her parting a trifle more lingering each time; so she was forced to speak the first—but women take the lead in such matters.

One evening, instead of offering her hand, she held up her cheek for a kiss. Pitou thought she had forgot, and was too honest to take advantage of a mistake.

But Catherine had not let go his hand, and she drew him closer to her. Seeing him still hesitate, little Isidore joined in, saying:

"Why won't you kiss Mamma Catherine, Papa Pitou?"

"Good gracious!" gasped Pitou, turning pale as if about to die, but letting his cold and trembling lip touch her cheek.

Taking the boy up, she put him in Pitou's arms, and said:

"I give you the boy, Ange; will you have the mother?"

This time, it was too much for the swain, whose head swam; he shut his eyes, and while he hugged the child, he dropped on a chair, and panted with the delicacy which only a delicate heart could appreciate:

"Oh, Master Isidore, how very fond I am of you!"

Isidore called Pitou "Papa Pitou," but Pitou called him "Master Isidore."

That is why, as he felt that love for her son had made Catherine love

Ange, he did not say:

"Oh, how dearly I love you, Catherine!"

This point settled that Pitou thought more of Isidore than of Catherine, they spoke of marriage.

"I don't want to seem in a hurry," said the man, "but if you mean to make me happy, do not be too long about it."

Catherine took a month.

At the end of three weeks Ange, in full regimentals, went respectfully to pay a visit to Aunt Angelique, with the aim to inform her of his near at hand union with Catherine Billet.

Seeing her nephew from afar, she hastened to shut her door. But he did not hold back from the inhospitable door whence he had once been expelled.

He rapped gently.

"Who is there?" snarled Angelique, in her sourest voice.

"I—your dutiful nephew, Ange Pitou."

"Go on your bloody way, you September man of massacre!" cried Aunt Angelique.

"Auntie, I come to tell you of a bit of news which can not fail to make you jolly, because it is my happiness."

"What is the news, you red-capped Jacobin?"

"I will tell you if you open the door."

"Say it through the door; I shall not open it to a breechless outlaw like you."

"If there is no other way, here you have it—I am going to get married."

The door flew open as by magic.

"Who are you going to marry, you wretched fellow?" asked the old spinster.

"Catherine Billet, please."

"Oh, the villain, the scamp, the regicide!" said the good soul; "he marries a ruined girl! Get you gone, scapegrace; I curse you!"

With a gesture quite noble, she held up her dry and yellow hands toward her nephew.

"Dear aunt," replied the young man, "you ought to know that I am too well hardened to your maledictions to care a fig for them. I only wanted to do the proper thing by inviting you to dance at my wedding; if you won't come, still I have asked you to shake a leg—"

"Shake a—fy, for shame!"

"Fare thee well, sweet Aunt Angelique!"

Touching his cocked hat in the military manner, Pitou made a salute to his relative and hurried away.

CHAPTER XXX. THE EFFECT OF HAPPY NEWS.

Pitou had to tell his intended marriage to Mayor Longpre, who lived hard by. Less set against the Billet family than Aunt 'Gelique, he congratulated Pitou on the match.

Pitou listened to his praise without seeing where he was doing very much of a noble action.

By the way, as a pure Republican, Pitou was delighted to find that the Republic had done away with the publication of the banns and other ecclesiastical trammels which had always galled true lovers.

It was, therefore, settled between the mayor and the suitor that the wedding should take place on the following Saturday, at the town hall.

Next day, Sunday, the sale of the Charny estate and the Billet farm was to come off. The latter, at the upset price of four hundred thousand and the other at six hundred thousand in paper money; assignats were dropping fearfully; the gold louis was worth nine hundred and twenty francs in paper.

But, then, nobody ever saw a gold piece nowadays.

Pitou had run all the way back to acquaint Catherine with the good news. He had ventured to anticipate the marriage-day by forty-eight hours, and he was afraid he should vex Catherine.

She did not appear vexed, and he was lifted up among the angels—his namesakes.

But she insisted on his going once more to Aunt Angelique's, to announce the exact date of the wedding-day and invite her to be at the ceremony. She was the bridegroom's sole relative, and though not at all tender toward him, he ought to do the proper thing on his side.

The consequence was that on Thursday morning, Pitou went over to Villers Cotterets to repeat the visit.

Nine o'clock was striking as he got in sight of the house.

The aunt was not on the door-step, but the door was closed any way, as if she expected his call.

He thought that she had stepped out, and he was delighted.

He would have paid the visit, and a polite note with a piece of wedding-cake after the ceremony would acquit the debt to courtesy.

Still, as he was a conscientious fellow, he went up to the door and knocked; as no answer came to his raps, he called.

At the double appeal of knuckle and voice, a neighbor appeared at her own door.

"Do you know whether or no my aunt has gone out, eh, Mother Fagot?" asked Pitou.

"Has she not answered?" asked Dame Fagot.

"No; she has not, as you see; so I guess she has gone out for a gossip."

Mother Fagot shook her head.

"I should have seen her go out," she said; "my door opens the same way as hers, and it is pretty seldom that in getting up of a morning she does not drop into our house to get some warm ashes to put in her shoes, with which the poor dear lamb keeps her toes warm all the day. Ain't that so, Neighbor Farolet?"

This question was addressed to a fresh character, who likewise opening his door, shoved his conversational oar into the parley.

"What are you talking about, Madame Fagot?"

"I was a-saying that Aunt Angelique had not gone out. Have you seen anything of her?"

"That I hain't, and I am open to wager that she has not gone out, otherwise her shutters would not be open, d'ye see."

"By all that is blue, that is true enough," remarked Pitou. "Heavens, I hope nothing unfortunate has happened to my poor aunt."

"I should not wonder," said Mother Fagot.

"It is more than possible, it is probable," said Farolet, sententiously.

"To tell the truth, she was not over-tender to me," went on Pitou; "but I do not want harm to befall her for all that. How are we going to find out the state of things?"

"That is not a puzzle," suggested a third neighbor, joining in; "send for Rigolot, the locksmith."

"If it is to open the door, he is not wanted," said Pitou; "I know a little trick of prying the bolt with a knife."

"Well, go ahead, my lad," said Farolet; "we are all witnesses that you picked the lock with the best intentions and your pocket-knife."

Pitou had taken out his knife, and in the presence of a dozen persons, attracted by the occurrence, he slipped back the bolt with a dexterity proving that he had used this means of opening the way more than once in his youth.

The door was open, but the interior was plunged into complete darkness. As the daylight gradually penetrated and was diffused, they could descry the form of the old girl on her bed.

Pitou called her by name twice. But she remained motionless and without response. He went in and up to the couch.

"Halloo!" he exclaimed, touching the hands; "she is cold and stark."

They opened the windows. Aunt Angelique was dead.

"What a misfortune!" said Pitou.

"Tush," said Farolet; "a hard winter is coming, and wood never so dear. She saves by departing where the firing is plentiful. Besides, your aunt did not dote on you."

"Maybe so," said Pitou, with tears as big as walnuts, "but I liked her

215

pretty well. Oh, my poor auntie!" said the big baby, falling on his knees by the bed.

"I say, Captain Pitou," said Mme. Fagot, "if you want anything, just let us know. If we ain't good neighbors, we ain't good for anything."

"Thank you, mother. Is that boy of yours handy?"

"Yes. Hey, Fagotin!" called the good woman.

A boy of fourteen stood frightened at the door.

"Here I am, mother," he said.

"Just bid him trot over to Haramont to tell Catherine not to be uneasy about me, as I have found my Aunt 'Gelique dead. Poor aunt!" He wiped away fresh tears. "That is what is keeping me here."

"You hear that, Fagotin? Then off you go."

"Go through Soissons Street," said the wise Farolet, "and notify Citizen Raynal that there is a case of sudden death to record at old Miss Pitou's."

The boy darted off on his double errand.

The crowd had kept increasing till there were a hundred before the door. Each had his own opinion on the cause of the decease, and all whispered among themselves.

"If Pitou is no fool, he will find some hoard smuggled away in an old sock, or in a crock, or in a hole in the chimney."

Dr. Raynal arrived in the midst of this, preceded by the head tax-gatherer.

The doctor went up to the bed, examined the corpse, and declared to the amaze of the lookers-on that the death was due to cold and starvation. This redoubled Pitou's tears.

"Oh, poor aunt!" he wailed, "and I thought she was so rich. I am a villain for having left her to poverty. Oh, had I only known this! It can not be, Doctor Raynal!"

"Look into the hutch and see if there is any bread; in the wood-box and see if there is any fire-wood. I have always foretold that the old miser would end in this way."

Searching, they found not a crumb or a splinter.

"Oh, why did she not tell me this?" mourned Pitou. "I would have chopped up some wood for her and done some poaching to fill the larder. It is your fault, too," the poor fellow added, accusing the crowd; "you ought to have told me that she was in want."

"We did not tell you that she was in want," returned wiseacre Farolet, "for the plain reason that everybody believed that she was rolling in riches."

Dr. Raynal had thrown the sheet over the cold face, and proceeded to the door, when Pitou intercepted him.

"Are you going, doctor?"

"Why, what more do you expect me to do here?"

"Then she is undoubtedly dead? Dear me, to die of cold and hunger, too!"

Raynal beckoned him.

"Boy, I am of the opinion that you should none the less seek high and low," he said.

"But, doctor, after your saying she died of want—"

"Misers have been known to die the same way, lying on their treasures. Hush!" he said, laying a finger on his lips, and going out-doors.

CHAPTER XXXI. THE EASY-CHAIR.

Pitou would have pondered more deeply on what the doctor told him, only he spied Catherine running up, with her boy in her arms.

Since there was no doubt that Aunt Angelique had died of privation, the eagerness of the neighbors to help her nephew had lessened. So Catherine arrived most timely. As she might be considered the wife of Pitou, it was her place to attend to his aunt, which the good creature set about doing with the same tenderness she had shown awhile before to her own mother.

Meanwhile, Pitou ran out to arrange for the funeral, which would be at two days' time, as the suddenness of the death compelled retention of the remains forty-eight hours. Religious ceremonies being suppressed for funerals as for marriages, he had only to do business with the sexton and the grave digger, after the mayor.

Before he departed, Catherine suggested that the marriage should be deferred for a day or two, as it would look strange for an act so important and joyous as a wedding to be performed on the same day as he conducted his aunt's remains to the cemetery.

"Besides, my dear, it is bad luck to have a wedding while a grave is open."

"Stuff," said Pitou; "from the moment I am your husband, I defy misfortune to get a grip on me."

"Dear Pitou, let us put it off till Monday," said the bride, holding up her hand to him; "you see that I am trying to make your wishes suit proprieties."

"But two days is a deuce of a long time, Catherine."

"Not when you have been waiting five years."

"A lot of things may happen in forty-eight hours," moaned Pitou.

"My falling off in love can not happen, Ange; and as you pretend that is the only thing in the world which concerns you—"

"Lord, yes, Catherine; the only—only thing!"

"Why, then, look here, Isidore, say to Papa Pitou: 'Do not be afraid, Papa Pitou; mamma loves you dearly, and will always love you.'"

The child repeated this in his pretty voice.

On this assurance, Pitou made no difficulty about going to the mayor's. He returned in about an hour, with all settled and paid for. With what money he had left he laid in a stock of wood and food for a couple of days.

It was high time that the firing had come into the old, weather-worn house, where the wind poured in at many a chink, and they might perish of cold. Pitou had found Catherine half frozen when he got back.

According to Catherine's wish, the marriage was postponed until Monday.

The intermediate time passed with the pair mourning by the death-bed.

Despite the huge fire Pitou kept roaring, the wind came in so sharp and chill that Pitou acknowledged that if his aunt had not died of hunger she must have been carried off by cold.

The time came for the removal of the corpse, the transit not taking long, as Aunt Angelique's dwelling adjoined the burial-ground.

All of that quarter and other representatives of the town went to the funeral, which Pitou and Catherine led as the chief mourners.

When the ceremony terminated, Pitou thanked those attending in his name and that of the dead, and they all filed before him, throwing holy water into the old maid's grave.

When left alone, Pitou looked round for Catherine, and saw her and Isidore kneeling on another grave where cypresses were planted. It was Mother Billet's. Pitou had dug those four cypresses in the woods and transplanted them. He did not care to disturb them in this pious occupation, but thinking that Catherine would be very cold at the end of her devotions, he determined to run on before and have a good fire blazing at her return.

Unfortunately, one thing opposed the realization of this good intention—they were out of wood. Pitou was in a pinch, for he was out of money, too.

He looked around him to see if there was nothing good to burn. There was Aunt Angelique's bread-safe, bed, and easy-chair. The bed and cupboard were not unworn, but they were still good; while the arm-chair was so rickety that nobody but the owner had ever risked themselves in it. It was therefore condemned.

Like the Revolutionary Tribunal, Pitou had no sooner condemned a thing than he proceeded to execute it.

Pitou set his knee to the seat, and seizing one of the sides, gave a pull. At the third of such tugs, it gave way at the joints. It uttered a kind of squeak, as if an animal capable of feeling pain and expressing emotion. If Pitou had been superstitious, he might have imagined that the aunt's spirit had located itself in her old arm-chair.

But Pitou had no superstition except his love for Catherine. This article of furniture was doomed to warm her, and though it had bled in each limb like an enchanted tree, it would have been rent to pieces.

He grasped the other arm with the same fierceness, and tore that from the carcass, which began to look dismantled.

Again the chair sent forth a sound strange and metallic.

Pitou remained insensible. He took up the chair by one leg, and swinging the whole round his head, he brought it down on the floor.

This split the seat in half, and to the great astonishment of the destroyer, out of the yawning chasm spouted torrents of gold.

Our readers will remember that it was Angelique's habit to change all her coppers into silver, and them into gold pieces, which she stowed away inside her chair.

When Pitou recovered from his surprise and dismay, his first impulse was to run out to Catherine and little Isidore and bring them in to view the riches he had discovered.

But the dreadful terror seized him that Catherine would not marry him if he were a rich man, and he shook his head.

"No," he said, "she would refuse me."

After reflecting for an instant, careworn and motionless, a smile passed over his face. No doubt he had hit on a means of surmounting the obstacle which this sudden wealth had raised. He gathered up the coin scattered on the floor and poked about in the cushion with his knife for still more of the golden eggs. They were literally crammed into the lining.

He reckoned, and there were fifteen hundred and fifty louis, otherwise, thirty-seven thousand and two hundred livres or francs, and at the discount in the favor of gold, he was the master of one million three hundred and twenty-six thousand livres!

And at what a moment had this slice of good luck befallen him! When he was obliged to smash up the furniture from having no means to buy fuel for his wife.

What a lucky thing that Pitou was so poor, the weather was so cold, and the old chair so rotten!

Who knows what would have happened but for this happy conjunction of circumstances?

He stuffed the coin away in all his pockets, and scraping the splinters together he built a fire, which he managed to kindle with the unused flint and steel.

He was no more than in time, for in came Catherine and little Isidore, shivering with cold.

Pitou gave the boy a hug, kissed the woman's icy hands, and dashed out, crying:

"Get warm. I have a piece of business to go through."

"Where does Papa Pitou go?" asked the boy.

"I do not know, but judging by the gait he is going at, it is for you or me."

She might have said, "For you and me."

CHAPTER XXXII. WHAT PITOU DID WITH THE FIND.

It has not been forgotten that the Charny estate and the Gilbert and Billet farms were in the market at a price. On the sale day, Mayor Longpre bought for "Mr. Cash" the properties at the price of 1,350 gold louis, for the equivalent of assignats.

This happened on Sunday, the eve of the day when Catherine and Pitou were married.

At eleven on the following day, all the crowd were grieving that a fine fellow like Pitou should throw himself away upon a girl who was ruined utterly, with a child who was even more poverty-stricken than herself.

When Mayor Longpre had pronounced Citizen Pierre Ange Pitou and Citizeness Anne Catherine Billet united in wedlock, he beckoned little Isidore to him. The youngster had been sitting upon the desk, whence he slipped down and came to him.

"My boy," he said, "here are some papers which you will please give your Mamma Catherine when Papa Pitou takes her home."

"Yes, sir," said the little fellow, taking two papers in his little hand.

All was finished, only, to the great astonishment of the spectators, Pitou pulled out five gold pieces and handed them to the mayor, saying:

"For the poor of the parish."

"Are we rich?" asked Catherine, smiling.

"Happy folks are always rich," returned Pitou, "and you have made me the happiest man in creation."

He offered his arm to the wife, who leaned on it affectionately.

On going forth, they found the crowd to which we have alluded.

Unanimous cheers greeted the couple. Pitou saluted his friends and gave many hand-shakes; Catherine nodded to hers and gave many smiles.

Pitou turned to the right.

"Why, where are you going, dearest?" asked Madame Pitou.

"Come, my dearly beloved," he replied, "to a place you will be glad to see again."

"Why, you are going toward our old farm," she said.

"Come on, all the same," he persisted.

"Oh, Pitou!" she sighed, as he brought her over the well-remembered way.

"And I thought to make you happy," he sighed, too.

"How could you think to make me happy by taking me again to a place which was my parents', and might have been mine, but which was sold yesterday to some stranger whose name even I do not know."

"Only a couple of steps farther; that is all I ask of you."

They turned the corner of the wall, and had the farm entrance before them.

All the farm-hands, carters, cow-men, dairy-maids, plowmen, were there, with Father Clovis marshaling them, a bunch of flowers in his hand.

"I understand; you wanted me to be welcomed once more in the old home by those who, like me, will leave it forever. I thank you, dear."

Leaving her husband's arm and Isidore's hand, she ran forward to meet the people, who surrounded her and bore her into the house.

Pitou led Isidore, who was still carrying the papers, into the door-way, and they saw Catherine seated in the main room, staring about her as in a dream.

"In Heaven's name, tell me what they are saying!" she cried. "I do not understand a bit of what they are saying."

"Perhaps these papers which the child has for you will make it all clear, dear Catherine," replied the husband.

She took the papers from the little hand, and read one by chance:

"I acknowledge that the manor-house of Boursonnes and the lands dependent were bought and paid for by me, yesterday, on behalf of Jacques Philip Isidore, minor son of Catherine Billet, and that consequently said house and lands are the property of the said son.

"LONGPRE, Mayor of Villers Cotterets."

"What does this mean, Pitou? You must understand that I can not make head or tail of it."

"Better read the other document," suggested the husband.

Unfolding the second paper, Catherine read as follows:

"I hereby acknowledge that the farm called Billet's, with the lands and buildings thereon and the appurtenances thereof, were bought and paid for by me, on behalf and for the account of Citizeness Anne Catherine Billet, and that it follows the said farm and lands and buildings belong to the said Citizeness Ann Catherine Billet.

"LONGPRE, Mayor of Villers Cotterets."

"In Heaven's name, tell me what this all means, or I shall go mad!" said Catherine.

"The meaning is," rejoined Pitou, "that thanks to some gold found in my Aunt Angelique's old easy-chair, which I broke up to warm you, the house and manor of Charny will not go out of the family, or the farm from the Billets."

Catherine understood all at last. She opened her arms to Pitou, but he pushed Isidore into them. But she leaned forward and infolded husband and child in the same embrace.

"Oh, God!" exclaimed Pitou, stifling with bliss and yet unable to repress one tear for the old maid, "to think there are people who die of hunger and cold, like poor Aunt Angelique!"

"Faith!" said a stout teamster, nudging a rosy milk-maid for her to take particular heed of their new master and mistress, "I do not think that pair is going to die in any such way."

Let us turn from these truly happy ones, in the peaceful country, to the bereaved widow of Louis XVI. In her lonesome jail she mourns over the loss of all—husband, lover, friend. What can replace a Charny or an Andrea? She thinks there is no champion of the blood of either, for she knows not that Cagliostro's surmise was not baseless. When the son of Andrea shall know how his mother fell, he will fly to arms to avenge that loss and to spite her foes, who are also the queen's! We shall trace his gallant, and desperate attempts to rescue the royal captive in the pages of the conclusion of this series, entitled: "The Knight of Redcastle: or, The Captivity of Marie Antoinette."

THE END

About Author

His father, General Thomas-Alexandre Dumas Davy de la Pailleterie, was born in the French colony of Saint-Domingue (present-day Haiti) to Alexandre Antoine Davy de la Pailleterie, a French nobleman, and Marie-Cessette Dumas, a black slave. At age 14 Thomas-Alexandre was taken by his father to France, where he was educated in a military academy and entered the military for what became an illustrious career.

Dumas' father's aristocratic rank helped young Alexandre acquire work with Louis-Philippe, Duke of Orléans, then as a writer, finding early success. Decades later, after the election of Louis-Napoléon Bonaparte in 1851, Dumas fell from favour and left France for Belgium, where he stayed for several years, then moved to Russia for a few years before going to Italy. In 1861, he founded and published the newspaper L'Indipendente, which supported Italian unification, before returning to Paris in 1864.

Though married, in the tradition of Frenchmen of higher social class, Dumas had numerous affairs (allegedly as many as forty). In his lifetime, he was known to have at least four illegitimate children; although twentieth-century scholars found that Dumas fathered three other children out of wedlock. He acknowledged and assisted his son, Alexandre Dumas, to become a successful novelist and playwright. They are known as Alexandre Dumas père ('father') and Alexandre Dumas fils ('son'). Among his affairs, in 1866, Dumas had one with Adah Isaacs Menken, an American actress then less than half his age and at the height of her career.

The English playwright Watts Phillips, who knew Dumas in his later life, described him as "the most generous, large-hearted being in the world. He also was the most delightfully amusing and egotistical creature on the face of the earth. His tongue was like a windmill – once set in motion, you never knew when he would stop, especially if the theme was himself."

Early life

Dumas Davy de la Pailleterie (later known as Alexandre Dumas) was born in 1802 in Villers-Cotterêts in the department of Aisne, in Picardy,

France. He had two older sisters, Marie-Alexandrine (born 1794) and Louise-Alexandrine (born 1796, died 1797). Their parents were Marie-Louise Élisabeth Labouret, the daughter of an innkeeper, and Thomas-Alexandre Dumas.

Thomas-Alexandre had been born in the French colony of Saint-Domingue (now Haiti), the mixed-race, natural son of the marquis Alexandre Antoine Davy de la Pailleterie, a French nobleman and général commissaire in the artillery of the colony, and Marie-Cessette Dumas, a slave of Afro-Caribbean ancestry. At the time of Thomas-Alexandre's birth, his father was impoverished. It is not known whether his mother was born in Saint-Domingue or in Africa, nor is it known from which African people her ancestors came.

Brought as a boy to France by his father and legally freed there, Thomas-Alexandre Dumas Davy was educated in a military school and joined the army as a young man. As an adult, Thomas-Alexandre used his mother's name, Dumas, as his surname after a break with his father. Dumas was promoted to general by the age of 31, the first soldier of Afro-Antilles origin to reach that rank in the French army. He served with distinction in the French Revolutionary Wars. He became general-in-chief of the Army of the Pyrenees, the first man of colour to reach that rank. Although a general under Bonaparte in the Italian and Egyptian campaigns, Dumas had fallen out of favour by 1800 and requested leave to return to France. On his return, his ship had to put in at Taranto in the Kingdom of Naples, where he and others were held as prisoners of war.

In 1806, when Alexandre was four years of age, his father, Thomas-Alexandre, died of cancer. His widowed mother, Marie-Louise, could not provide her son with much of an education, but Dumas read everything he could and taught himself Spanish. Although poor, the family had their father's distinguished reputation and aristocratic rank to aid the children's advancement. In 1822, after the restoration of the monarchy, the 20-year-old Alexandre Dumas moved to Paris. He acquired a position at the Palais Royal in the office of Louis-Philippe, Duke of Orléans.

Career

While working for Louis-Philippe, Dumas began writing articles for magazines and plays for the theatre. As an adult, he used his slave grandmother's surname of Dumas, as his father had done as an adult. His first play, Henry III and His Courts, produced in 1829 when he was 27 years old, met with acclaim. The next year, his second play, Christine, was equally popular. These successes gave him sufficient income to write full-time.

In 1830, Dumas participated in the Revolution that ousted Charles X and replaced him with Dumas' former employer, the Duke of Orléans, who ruled as Louis-Philippe, the Citizen King. Until the mid-1830s, life in France remained unsettled, with sporadic riots by disgruntled Republicans and impoverished urban workers seeking change. As life slowly returned to normal, the nation began to industrialise. An improving economy combined with the end of press censorship made the times rewarding for Alexandre Dumas' literary skills.

After writing additional successful plays, Dumas switched to writing novels. Although attracted to an extravagant lifestyle and always spending more than he earned, Dumas proved to be an astute marketer. As newspapers were publishing many serial novels, in 1838, Dumas rewrote one of his plays as his first serial novel, Le Capitaine Paul. He founded a production studio, staffed with writers who turned out hundreds of stories, all subject to his personal direction, editing, and additions.

From 1839 to 1841, Dumas, with the assistance of several friends, compiled Celebrated Crimes, an eight-volume collection of essays on famous criminals and crimes from European history. He featured Beatrice Cenci, Martin Guerre, Cesare and Lucrezia Borgia, as well as more recent events and criminals, including the cases of the alleged murderers Karl Ludwig Sand and Antoine François Desrues, who were executed.

Dumas collaborated with Augustin Grisier, his fencing master, in his 1840 novel, The Fencing Master. The story is written as Grisier's account of how he came to witness the events of the Decembrist revolt in Russia. The novel was eventually banned in Russia by Czar Nicholas I, and Dumas was prohibited from visiting the country until after the Czar's death. Dumas refers to Grisier with great respect in The Count of Monte Cristo, The Corsican

Brothers, and in his memoirs.

Dumas depended on numerous assistants and collaborators, of whom Auguste Maquet was the best known. It was not until the late twentieth century that his role was fully understood. Dumas wrote the short novel Georges (1843), which uses ideas and plots later repeated in The Count of Monte Cristo. Maquet took Dumas to court to try to get authorial recognition and a higher rate of payment for his work. He was successful in getting more money, but not a by-line.

Dumas' novels were so popular that they were soon translated into English and other languages. His writing earned him a great deal of money, but he was frequently insolvent, as he spent lavishly on women and sumptuous living. (Scholars have found that he had a total of 40 mistresses.) In 1846, he had built a country house outside Paris at Le Port-Marly, the large Château de Monte-Cristo, with an additional building for his writing studio. It was often filled with strangers and acquaintances who stayed for lengthy visits and took advantage of his generosity. Two years later, faced with financial difficulties, he sold the entire property.

Dumas wrote in a wide variety of genres and published a total of 100,000 pages in his lifetime. He also made use of his experience, writing travel books after taking journeys, including those motivated by reasons other than pleasure. Dumas traveled to Spain, Italy, Germany, England and French Algeria. After King Louis-Philippe was ousted in a revolt, Louis-Napoléon Bonaparte was elected president. As Bonaparte disapproved of the author, Dumas fled in 1851 to Brussels, Belgium, which was also an effort to escape his creditors. About 1859, he moved to Russia, where French was the second language of the elite and his writings were enormously popular. Dumas spent two years in Russia and visited St. Petersburg, Moscow, Kazan, Astrakhan and Tbilisi, before leaving to seek different adventures. He published travel books about Russia.

In March 1861, the kingdom of Italy was proclaimed, with Victor Emmanuel II as its king. Dumas travelled there and for the next three years participated in the movement for Italian unification. He founded and led a newspaper, Indipendente. While there, he befriended Giuseppe Garibaldi, whom he had long admired and with whom he shared a commitment to liberal republican principles as well as membership within Freemasonry. Returning to Paris in 1864, he published travel books about Italy.

Despite Dumas' aristocratic background and personal success, he had to deal with discrimination related to his mixed-race ancestry. In 1843, he wrote a short novel, Georges, that addressed some of the issues of race and the effects of colonialism. His response to a man who insulted him about his African ancestry has become famous. Dumas said:

My father was a mulatto, my grandfather was a Negro, and my great-grandfather a monkey. You see, Sir, my family starts where yours ends.

Personal life

On 1 February 1840, Dumas married actress Ida Ferrier (born Marguerite-Joséphine Ferrand) (1811–1859). He had numerous liaisons with other women and was known to have fathered at least four children by them:

Alexandre Dumas, fils (1824–1895), son of Marie-Laure-Catherine Labay (1794–1868), a dressmaker. He became a successful novelist and playwright.

Marie-Alexandrine Dumas (5 March 1831 – 1878), the daughter of Belle Krelsamer (1803–1875).

Micaëlla-Clélie-Josepha-Élisabeth Cordier (born 1860), the daughter of Emélie Cordier.

Henry Bauer, the son of a woman whose surname was Bauer.

About 1866, Dumas had an affair with Adah Isaacs Menken, a well-known American actress. She had performed her sensational role in Mazeppa in London. In Paris, she had a sold-out run of Les Pirates de la Savanne and was at the peak of her success.

These women were among Dumas' nearly 40 mistresses found by scholar Claude Schopp, in addition to three natural children.

Death and legacy

At his death in December 1870, Dumas was buried at his birthplace of Villers-Cotterêts in the department of Aisne. His death was overshadowed by the Franco-Prussian War. Changing literary fashions decreased his popularity. In the late twentieth century, scholars such as Reginald Hamel and Claude Schopp have caused a critical reappraisal and new appreciation of his art, as well as finding lost works.

In 1970, the Alexandre Dumas Paris Métro station was named in his honour. His country home outside Paris, the Château de Monte-Cristo, has been restored and is open to the public as a museum.

Researchers have continued to find Dumas works in archives, including the five-act play, The Gold Thieves, found in 2002 by the scholar Réginald Hamel [fr] in the Bibliothèque Nationale de France. It was published in France in 2004 by Honoré-Champion.

Frank Wild Reed (1874–1953), the older brother of Dunedin publisher A. H. Reed, was a busy Whangarei pharmacist who never visited France, yet he amassed the greatest collection of books and manuscripts relating to Dumas outside France. It contains about 3350 volumes, including some 2000 sheets in Dumas' handwriting and dozens of French, Belgian and English first editions. This collection was donated to Auckland Libraries after his death. Reed wrote the most comprehensive bibliography of Dumas.

In 2002, for the bicentennial of Dumas' birth, French President Jacques Chirac had a ceremony honouring the author by having his ashes re-interred at the mausoleum of the Panthéon of Paris, where many French luminaries were buried. The proceedings were televised: the new coffin was draped in a blue velvet cloth and carried on a caisson flanked by four mounted Republican Guards costumed as the four Musketeers. It was transported through Paris to the Panthéon. In his speech, President Chirac said:

With you, we were D'Artagnan, Monte Cristo, or Balsamo, riding along the roads of France, touring battlefields, visiting palaces and castles—with you, we dream.

Chirac acknowledged the racism that had existed in France and said that the re-interment in the Pantheon had been a way of correcting that wrong, as Alexandre Dumas was enshrined alongside fellow great authors Victor Hugo and Émile Zola. Chirac noted that although France has produced many great writers, none has been so widely read as Dumas. His novels have been translated into nearly 100 languages. In addition, they have inspired more than 200 motion pictures.

In June 2005, Dumas' last novel, The Knight of Sainte-Hermine, was published in France featuring the Battle of Trafalgar. Dumas described a fictional character killing Lord Nelson (Nelson was shot and killed by an unknown sniper). Writing and publishing the novel serially in 1869, Dumas had nearly finished it before his death. It was the third part of the Sainte-Hermine trilogy.

Claude Schopp, a Dumas scholar, noticed a letter in an archive in 1990 that led him to discover the unfinished work. It took him years to research it, edit the completed portions, and decide how to treat the unfinished part. Schopp finally wrote the final two-and-a-half chapters, based on the author's notes, to complete the story. Published by Éditions Phébus, it sold 60,000 copies, making it a best seller. Translated into English, it was released in 2006 as The Last Cavalier, and has been translated into other languages.

Schopp has since found additional material related to the Saints-Hermine saga. Schopp combined them to publish the sequel Le Salut de l'Empire in 2008.

Dumas is briefly mentioned in the 1994 film The Shawshank Redemption. The inmate Heywood mispronounces Dumas' last name as "dumbass" as he files books in the prison library.

Dumas is briefly mentioned in the 2012 film Django Unchained. The Southern slaveholder Calvin Candie expressed admiration for Dumas, owning his books in his library and even naming one of his slaves D'Artagnan. He is surprised to learn from another white man that Dumas was black. (Source: Wikipedia)

CPSIA information can be obtained
at www.ICGtesting.com
Printed in the USA
BVHW081024020919

557347BV00008BA/312/P